APACHE CUNNING

The onrushing Apache's last cry was torn from his throat as Jock's bullet smashed into his chest, ripping through arteries and heart like some metal fist.

Jock levered another cartridge into the rifle's chamber and got to his feet, expecting more Apaches to rush him. Instead, he saw a gaggle of ponies racing off to the south.

"Looks like you chased them off," Beeson said.

"I didn't chase them off, Amos. This one came after me and I shot him. I think he sacrificed his life so that the others could escape."

"Them murderin' bastards knew they was outnumbered. If we'd have got here in time, we'd have turned all of them cowardly savages into wolf meat."

"I don't think they ran because of cowardice," Jock said. "I think they had other things on their mind."

Ralph Compton

The
Ellsworth Trail

A Ralph Compton Novel
by Jory Sherman

A SIGNET BOOK

SIGNET
Published by New American Library, a division of
Penguin Group (USA) Inc., 375 Hudson Street,
New York, New York 10014, USA
Penguin Group (Canada), 90 Eglinton Avenue East, Suite 700, Toronto,
Ontario M4P 2Y3, Canada (a division of Pearson Penguin Canada Inc.)
Penguin Books Ltd., 80 Strand, London WC2R 0RL, England
Penguin Ireland, 25 St. Stephen's Green, Dublin 2,
Ireland (a division of Penguin Books Ltd.)
Penguin Group (Australia), 250 Camberwell Road, Camberwell, Victoria 3124,
Australia (a division of Pearson Australia Group Pty. Ltd.)
Penguin Books India Pvt. Ltd., 11 Community Centre, Panchsheel Park,
New Delhi - 110 017, India
Penguin Group (NZ), cnr Airborne and Rosedale Roads, Albany,
Auckland 1310, New Zealand (a division of Pearson New Zealand Ltd.)
Penguin Books (South Africa) (Pty.) Ltd., 24 Sturdee Avenue,
Rosebank, Johannesburg 2196, South Africa

Penguin Books Ltd., Registered Offices:
80 Strand, London WC2R 0RL, England

First published by Signet, an imprint of New American Library,
a division of Penguin Group (USA) Inc.

First Printing, December 2005
10 9 8 7 6 5 4 3 2 1

THE IMMORTAL COWBOY

This is respectfully dedicated to the "American Cowboy." His was the saga sparked by the turmoil that followed the Civil War, and the passing of more than a century has by no means diminished the flame.

True, the old days and the old ways are but treasured memories, and the old trails have grown dim with the ravages of time, but the spirit of the cowboy lives on.

In my travels—to Texas, Oklahoma, Kansas, Nebraska, Colorado, Wyoming, New Mexico, and Arizona—I always find something that reminds me of the Old West. While I am walking these plains and mountains for the first time, there is this feeling that a part of me is eternal, that I have known these old trails before. I believe it is the undying spirit of the frontier calling, allowing me, through the mind's eye, to step back into time. What is the appeal of the Old West of the American frontier?

It has been epitomized by some as the dark and bloody period in American history. Its heroes—Crockett, Bowie, Hickok, Earp—have been reviled and criticized. Yet the Old West lives on, larger than life.

It has become a symbol of freedom, when there was always another mountain to climb and another river to cross; when a dispute between two men was settled not with expensive lawyers, but with fists, knives, or guns. Barbaric? Maybe. But some things never change. When the cowboy rode into the pages of American history, he left behind a legacy that lives within the hearts of us all.

—*Ralph Compton*

Chapter 1

The smoke from his cigarette scratched at his eyes, burning them like shaven onions would. His tear ducts welled up and spilled over, washing away some of the grit, the fine dust that rose off the land like tiny insects that lived with the Texas wind and died on his flesh, on his lips, in his mouth, under the faded blue bandanna around his neck, and in the fluted scallops of his ears. The cigarette dangled from his dry and cracked lips like some limp brown cocoon, the once-white paper as scorched and dusty as the land he rode upon, a dangling appendage burning like a fuse attached to a stick of dynamite.

The anger had not lessened in him since he rode out of Del Rio and followed the meandering course of the Nueces River south toward Corpus Christi. His rage was fueled by memories of what he had lost, what he was leaving behind, and by the poignant ache inside him for the land, all of it, all that was now gone, and all that lay ahead. Each mile he put behind him reminded him of the land that had once been, the land that had once been his. For it was the same land, most of the way. It did not change that much, not in that dimension of mind where memory's universe resides, not in the depths of his heart.

But the land did change after he forded the Nueces and rode into high grass and the smell of sweet clover and lespedeza, and the musty aroma of alfalfa, the wildflowers gone or smothered by green blades of X8 grass planted long ago by his far-seeing friend with the green thumb.

He saw the horseman long before the lone rider saw him. He knew somehow that the man was waiting for someone because he did not move from his spot on a knoll, but sat his standing horse like a sentinel, some guardian of an invisible gate to a kingdom beyond sight, beyond the comprehension of a man who had ridden a trail through desolation and emptiness of both sky and land.

The man had turned away to swat at a fly or some other winged creature, but when he turned his head, he looked directly toward the ford where a man would come from the west if a man were to come to these vast grasslands.

The man stood up in his stirrups and pushed his hat back as if to give his eyes more scope. Beyond him, longhorns grazed in bunches, their sweeping horns glinting like slashing sabers in the sun. The cattle smell mingled with the other scents and tugged at the rider's heart, pulling on memories like wet leather thongs tied there, drying and tautening until they would twang if plucked.

"Ho there," the sentinel called. "You yonder."

The man waited as the rider from Del Rio approached, the cigarette stuck to his lips gone to ash and dead in the wind because he had not puffed on it for those moments when his horse was picking its way across the river, his legs quivering in the current until the hide rippled over the bones.

"Are you Jock Kane?" the guardian asked.

"I am."

"Mr. Becker told me to look for you. He said you'd be coming." The man glanced at the black armband on Kane's left sleeve, then averted his gaze as if he had violated some privacy.

Jock spat the stub of the cigarette from his mouth and licked the stuck paper on his lips until it loosened. He wiped his lower lip and reached into his left-hand shirt pocket for the makings. He pulled out the sack of tobacco, cranked one leg up and draped it over the saddle horn. He fished a packet of cigarette papers from the same pocket, slid one free of the sheaf, then stuffed the packet back into his pocket. He curled the single sheet of thin paper around his left index finger and loosened the string on the pouch, which opened into a small pucker. He poured the tobacco evenly into the paper, shook it slightly to even it all up, then, between thumb and index finger, rolled what he had into a tightly packed cigarette. He licked the top edge to seal it and stuck the quirly into his mouth. He pulled the string to close the pouch and stuck that back in his pocket.

The cowhand searched his pockets for a match to light Jock's cigarette. When he looked up, Jock was striking a lucifer on his trousers leg. The match burst into flame and Jock touched it to the end of his cigarette. The paper fumed and the spark ignited the tobacco as he pulled air through it.

"And where is Chad?" Jock asked, blowing

out a plume of blue smoke from one corner of his mouth.

"I'll take you to him. He ain't at home."

Jock looked at the cattle, turning his head so that the smoke didn't burn his eyes. There were cattle grazing in herds that stretched to every horizon. He couldn't see the brands from that distance, but he would bet good money, if he had any, that they all bore the X8 brand. It was well past spring roundup, so what was Chad doing out in the field counting head?

"Do it, then," Jock said. "You got a name?"

"Yes, sir. I'm Jesse. Jesse Boyd."

"How old are you, son?"

"I'm seventeen."

Jock snorted. Boyd's pale face was mottled with freckles that stretched from cheek to cheek over the bridge of his nose. His blue eyes had no clouds of age in them—innocent eyes that could still light up with wonder at the sight of a calf birthing, or a morning glory opening its petals to the sun.

"Almost," Boyd said. "In a couple of months."

"Lead on out, Boyd." The cigarette in Jock's mouth bobbed up and down when he spoke, like a flagless semaphore staff. Boyd's eyes fixated on it so that he stared like someone hypnotized by a snake.

"Yes, sir. Follow me."

Boyd turned his horse and rode down off the knoll, his small, thin body bobbing in the saddle so that he looked as if he were made of straw—a skinny scarecrow of a boy in man's clothing.

More and more cattle appeared before them as they rode. Jock got the distinct impression that the herd was thickening in size like something growing before his very eyes. The grass shortened, and disgruntled longhorns stood disconsolate on overgrazed earth, looking forlorn and mean, with their brown eyes glaring at him as he passed, as if inflicting silent blame on him for something he'd done, or hadn't done. These cattle, he thought, are going to kill something, anyone on two legs stupid enough to get close to those deadly horns.

Jock's uneasiness increased as the young man led them through milling longhorns and he saw riders circling them, so far off that he could not see their faces. They were just dark figures that looked like centaurs, each half horse, half man, with no definition that might have separated them. Men controlling a huge herd of cattle, getting ready for something, something that Jock dreaded knowing about, even in the hollow recesses of his heart where so much had been torn out, smashed, thrown away like dead meat.

"Mr. Becker's just up ahead," Boyd said, looking back at Jock. "That's him about to throw his loop."

Jock saw Chad chasing after a steer, swinging a manila rope over his head as he closed the gap between his horse and the moving target. He might have sprung from some olden tableau, painted during the early days of Texas when the longhorns were as wild as lions on an African veldt, rulers of a kingdom where they were the dominant animal, unchallenged except for a few Apaches with a taste for beef.

Becker threw his loop and it encircled the neck of the steer, falling gracefully over its head despite the longhorns that made such a feat remarkable. Chad's horse skidded to a stiff-legged stop and began to back up, taking the slack out of the rope. When the steer hit the end of its tether, it gyrated and flew to the ground as the horse backed down to a sitting position on its haunches—a rock holding a thrashing fish on the end of a line.

Boyd and Kane rode up as hands rushed to pin down the steer, while another waddled bowlegged up to it with a hot branding iron.

"I see you haven't lost your touch, Chad," Jock said. "You rope pretty good for an old man."

Chad looked over at Jock as he urged his mount toward the downed steer, pulling in the slack so that he could retrieve his lariat once the hands were finished burning the X8 into the steer's hide. Jock smelled the acrid fumes of hair and flesh, heard the soft hiss of the iron as it blazed its owner's mark on the cow's hip.

"Look who's calling who old," Chad said, his grin widening to show his teeth. "Surprised you ain't got a gray beard, Jocko."

The two men had not seen much of each other since right after the war, but they had kept in touch by mail. They had both come home after serving in the Second Texas Regiment, built their ranches and started herds, then split up, with Jock going to Del Rio, where he was from, and Chad returning to Corpus Christi, where he had been raised. They had formed strong bonds with each other during the fighting in the War Between the States.

"That's why I shave, Chad. The hairs have started coming up gray for some reason."

The hands finished with the branded steer and turned it loose. The steer ran bawling into the sea of longhorns that seemed packed together as though they were in a loading chute with enormous dimensions. Chad coiled his rope and tied its garland to his saddle with a leather thong. The men around them all stared at Jock Kane, sizing him up. He looked at them but made no effort toward friendliness. He just returned their stares, one by one, and then looked back at Chad.

"Come on, Jock. Follow me," Chad said. "We've got some talking to do."

Jock nodded. He saw resentment gather on some of the men's faces, like moss growing at the base of a tree deep in a forest. He understood that. He was the outsider, the stranger. They didn't know him and he didn't know them. They had their suspicions and he had his.

The bunched cattle parted, reluctantly, to let the two riders through. When they were some distance away from the men and had a clear spot near some mesquite trees, Chad stopped, turned his horse. Jock's cigarette tip glowed as he drew smoke into his lungs.

"That was the last one we had to brand, Jock."

"You've built yourself quite a herd, Chad.

I'm just wondering if you brought me out here to brag or if you had something else in mind."

"Jock, I'm damned sorry about Twyla. I see you're still wearing crepe."

"It's not crepe. It's cloth."

"You know what I mean. I wanted to come to the funeral, but I had my hands full."

"That's all right. I buried her, and I'll wear this black band on my arm until I get the bastard who murdered her."

"You know who it is?"

"I do."

"Vengeance is mine, sayeth—"

Jock broke in. "I've heard it all, Chad, and wrestled with it. When the Lord doesn't step in, then a man has to do the job. Vengeance will be mine. And Twyla's."

"All right, Jock."

"I still don't know why I rode all the way from Del Rio. You said it was urgent. I don't see any urgent hereabouts."

"Jock, I've got fifteen thousand head of longhorns ready to drive up to Ellsworth. I want you to be my trail boss."

Jock took the stub of the cigarette out of his mouth and drew in a deep breath. He stared hard at Chad, eye to eye, a flexing scowl on his face as if he were ready to lash out with both fists and knock Chad from his horse.

"You're crazy, Chad."

"No. I've given it a lot of thought. You're the only one I'd trust to get these cattle to the railhead in Ellsworth."

"The answer is no. I learned my lesson."

"When you fall off a horse, you get back up and ride it."

"Not this horse."

"Come to the house for supper. I don't give up that easy."

"Neither do I, Chad. Good luck with your herd. I'll ride on back home in the morning."

A look passed between the two men. They knew each other. They had been through hell together in a half dozen bloody battles.

"Is it Twyla's killer, Jock? You think he'll go back to Del Rio?"

"No, I don't think he'll go back there."

"Why not? Why are you so sure, Jocko?"

"Didn't you hear, Chad? Didn't you hear who raped and murdered my Twyla?"

Chad shook his head. "No, I reckon not. News travels slow down this way."

Jock pulled out the makings and built himself another cigarette. He lit it and blew smoke into the long silence. There was no expression on his face. It was like an empty sky, devoid of all life, just something that might have been painted with an undercoating, waiting for the painter to put life to it.

"It was my brother, Chad. Abel killed Twyla."

Chad's face froze into a rigid mask as if the breath had been sucked out of him and all that remained was a lifeless shell.

Chapter 2

Chad opened his mouth to speak, but his first utterance was a long, soulful gasp as if he were expiring on the spot. Blood drained from his face and, for a moment, Jock thought the man was going to have some kind of a fit, or worse, suffer a stroke. The shock, he decided, was genuine.

"Chad?"

Another long moment passed before Chad found his voice. The first sentence, however, came out as a gravelly croak, as if he were being throttled by an invisible hand.

"Did I hear you right, Jock? Abel killed Twyla? No, that can't be."

Twyla. The sound of her name made Jock wince inside as if he had been stung by a hornet unexpectedly. Twyla, so frail, so delicate, so fragile, like bone china or a tiny humming-bird. Twyla, with her elfin face, her long, raven black hair, her oversized blue eyes set like sapphires in almond-shaped depressions in her alabaster flesh. At times she looked almost transparent, when the sun was just right and she was wearing a pale dress, her skin so thin it seemed translucent, seemed he could see pure crystal bones just underneath. She was like something fashioned out of glass by a sculptor with loving hands. At times she seemed like a tiny fawn that never grew to size, a shy creature of the woods, dappled by sunlight in a grove of green-leafed trees.

"Twyla had rheumatic fever when she was a child. It did something to her heart, I guess. Made it weak, the doc said. It just gave out when Abel did what he did."

"He violated her?"

Jock winced visibly.

"He was drunk. Took after her when I was gone. I got back home and he was on top of her. I would have killed him right then, but Twyla was gasping for breath like a fish out of water. That bastard run out buck naked and Twyla died in my arms. God, Chad, it just crushed me. To see her die like that. To see what Abel had done to her, the bastard."

"I didn't know, Jock. I'm real sorry."

Neither man spoke for a few minutes. Jock puffed on his cigarette, but did not take it from his mouth. He stared at all the cattle until they blurred into one mottled blob of colors, their horns like a jumble of bones.

"Abel come by here a couple of weeks ago, Jock," Chad said quietly.

"What?"

"I didn't know what he'd done. He borrowed some money from me. He was with two rowdies I never saw before. They looked like three hardcases and I was glad to get rid of them."

"Was Abel drunk?"

"Nope. When I asked him about you, he just said you were in mourning, doing poorly."

"You gave him money? Where was he going?"

"Said he was hooking up with an outfit north of here. Didn't say who. Didn't say where."

"Do you know the names of the boys he was riding with?"

"One was called Randy. Randy Clutter. The other'n was older. Name of D.F. That's all the other two called him."

"Dan Fogarty," Jock said. "I warned Abel about him. He's a no-account."

"Looked like a real hardcase to me."

"He is. So is Randy. Those boys never did an honest day's work in their lives."

"Why did Abel take up with them?" Chad asked.

"It's a long story, Chad."

"Yeah, we don't need to talk about these things now. Have some chuck with us tonight and we'll chew the fat afterward. I really want you to take this herd up to Ellsworth for me."

"Ellsworth?"

"I've got an offer. Forty dollars a head on the hoof."

Jock blew a low whistle out of the side of his mouth.

"How many head you taking up, Chad?"

Chad waited several seconds for dramatic effect. "Better'n fifteen thousand head, Jock."

Jock took the cigarette from between his lips and squinched it out in his bare fist, thumbing it to so much tobacco and paper detritus in the palm of his hand. Then he opened his hand and let the debris fall to the breeze, which danced into nothingness.

"Have you lost all your senses, Chad? What happened to me could happen to you."

"I've thought about that. You lost everything you had. Twelve thousand dollars, wasn't it?"

"That much. More, really."

"Bad luck."

"No, Chad. Not all bad luck. Though I had enough of it. Indians ragged us all the way to the Red. We lost cattle crossing the river. Kansas farmers used us for target practice. More Indians, robbing us blind. And then that damned hailstorm."

"What was that like?" Chad asked.

"It was hell. Hailstones the size of a boy's fist came down with the velocity of cannon-balls. Cattle dropped like stoned rabbits. Our horses, some of my men. There was no shelter, no getting away from any of it. It was like a war and we couldn't fight back. Those of us who made it hid under dead horses and dead cows."

"A fluke of nature," Chad said.

"Well, nature's a big enemy on a cattle drive. What I had left after the hailstorm was taken away by three twisters in the same week. Winds that blew the clothes off your back, picked up cows and horses and men and tossed them back down like rag dolls a mile away. Stuff flying through the air that would cut you to ribbons. One of my boys had his head sliced off by a chunk of lumber. Clean decapitated him while he was riding his horse. His head screamed and I can still see his eyes staring at me as his skull thumped on the ground. His body didn't fall off for another ten yards and then flapped on the ground like a chicken with its head cut off. You don't forget those things, Chad. You don't ever forget them."

"You lost your ranch, I know."

"I lost everything I had. And then I lost Twyla. I'm a beaten man, Chad. I wouldn't drive a cow to the milk barn, much less go back to Kansas."

"The Jock I knew in the war never gave up."

"I'm not the same Jock."

"Yes, you are. You're not a quitter, Jock."

Jock shook his head, built another cigarette. It was what he did these days. Build cigarettes, smoke them, try not to think of the past, the war, the disastrous cattle drive to Abilene, the death of his wife, the treachery of his brother. He tried to turn these memories into smoke, but they remained like burning ashes, like smoldering coals in his mind, tormenting him, ruining his sleep, wrecking his days.

"Have you got enough men for this drive, Chad? With that many head you'll need at least . . ."

"Sixty men, I figure. I got that many. Two chuck wagons, special built. Some damned good wranglers and enough good drovers to teach the new ones."

"You're biting off a lot to chew. I drove three thousand head up north and had my hands plumb full."

"That's why I know you'd make me a fine trail boss. You've been over the trail and you know what can happen. Those of us here are all tenderfeet."

"I said no, Chad. And I mean it."

Chad didn't argue with Jock, nor did he say anything just then.

The men who had been at the branding began to mount up after putting out the fire and cooling the irons. Some of them looked over at Chad and Jock. Chad nodded to them.

"Come on, Jock. Let's go get some grub. You might know some of the boys."

"If I do, I probably owe them money," Jock said.

Chapter 3

Jock sniffed the air as he and Chad rode toward the chuck wagon, following the hands who had done the branding. The aroma of beef and vegetables, likely in a stew, he thought, assailed his nostrils and made his stomach rumble with hunger. It had been some time since he had eaten well and there had been days when he had not eaten at all.

"Hungry?" Chad said, as the chuck wagon appeared just on the horizon ahead.

"I could eat the south end of a northbound horse," Jock said.

"You'll have to settle for beef. Do you know Jubilee?"

"The cookie at the Flying W? He was old when I was a boy. I thought he was dead."

"He's not as old as he looks. He's my main cook. I thought you might remember him."

"At roundup, he was a godsend. Jubal Lee Daggett."

Chad laughed. "You do remember him, old Jubal Lee."

"Who could forget him?"

"Well, you're going to eat his grub tonight," he said.

As they drew close to the chuck wagon, Jock could hear the clank of utensils, the throaty, muscular conversation of hungry men. Some riders leaned down and drew their arms back, holding something edible before they rode back out to the pastures, their faces as dusted as Jock's, their shirts black with sweat.

In the distance, Jock heard the *screee, screee* squeal of seagulls and, when he looked up, he saw wings flashing white in the sunlight, like someone's fresh-washed laundry floating on invisible currents of air. Corpus Christi over the horizon, and the Gulf of Mexico, the green, white-capped sea carrying ships in and out of port—another world, one he had not seen in a long time.

Men sat on the ground holding tin plates with raised edges that resembled large, narrow bowls. The plates were filled with stew and, on some, biscuits of hardtack floated like islands. The talk died down when Chad and Jock rode up and dismounted.

Jock saw Jubilee look up from his serving table. His face cracked open with a toothless grin. His ginger hair sprouted out from a faded bandanna in little, wiry sprigs. The bandanna was wrapped around his head like a turban, hiding the bald spots—most of them. His apron looked almost edible with its streaks of gravy and splotches of unidentifiable vegetables.

"Wal," Daggett said, "if it ain't Jock Kane, after all these years. All growed up and haired over."

"Howdy, Jubal Lee," Jock said. "You're as ageless as a live oak."

The two shook hands quickly.

The men sitting around all looked at Kane, some of them disapprovingly.

"Get yourself a plate, Jocko," Jubilee said.

There was a young man standing next to the cook. He handed Jock a plate.

"I'm Mac," he said, "Jubilee's helper. I sure heard a lot about you, Mr. Kane."

"Never mind, Mac," Jubilee said. He ladled Jock's plate full of the thick stew. The aroma made Jock's stomach roil once again with hunger contractions.

"A lot of folks heard about you, Kane," a man sitting apart from the others said.

Mac handed Jock a big spoon and put a piece of hardtack on his plate, sticking it into the stew like a miniature tombstone.

Jock turned around, looked at the man who had spoken to him.

"Don't pay him no mind, Jock," Chad whispered, stepping up to the serving table.

But Jock ignored Chad and walked over to the man who had made the remark, Lou Quist.

"What do you mean by that, Quist?" Jock asked.

Quist, a wiry stub of a man, whose neck was as thick as his head, with sloping shoulders and muscled arms that stretched the fabric of his sleeves, looked up at Jock and squinted one eye as if trying to shut out some of the sunlight and focus on Jock, like a bird eyeing a night crawler.

"I mean, you got yourself quite a reputation, Jocko. Everybody's heard about Jock Kane."

"Heard what?" Jock said.

"Well, now, I'm not a man to repeat idle gossip. But you got a mark on you, Kane, just like your namesake in the Bible."

Chad stepped up, carrying his full plate. He scowled to show his annoyance with the way the conversation was turning. "That's enough of that, Lou. Watch your tongue. We're all friends here."

"Kane ain't no friend of mine," Quist said. "He owes me six months' pay, plus the cost of two horses."

"How do you figure?" Jock asked.

"I was drovin' those three thousand head up to Abilene, remember? The ones you was going to pay us with. And I lost two good horses in that hailstorm."

"You can't lay no blame on Jock for that storm, Lou," Chad said.

"Like hell I can't." Lou's face was turning a pale rose in the sun, as if the light had daubed him with pastel chalk. "He drove us right into that sonofabitch, the sky black as hell, lightning dancing ahead of us."

Quist got to his feet, leaving his dish on the ground. He was at least a half foot shorter than Jock, but the rest of him made up for it in width. His neck thickened with the rage building inside him and he licked his lips like a man spoiling for a fight.

"I don't owe you a damned cent, Quist," Jock said. "When you signed on with me, the agreement was you'd be paid if and when we got the cattle to market in Abilene. We all lost on that deal."

"I don't figure it that way, Kane."

Jock turned to Chad, handing him his plate of food. "Hold this for me, will you, Chad?"

Then Jock unstrapped his gunbelt, rebuckled it and handed it to another man standing close by. None of the men, including Lou Quist, were wearing sidearms.

"Figure it any way you want, Quist," Jock said, "but we didn't get the cattle to market and none of us got paid. Some of us lost more than others, more than you."

"I work for a man, I expect to get paid."

"You worked for yourself," Jock said. "I just provided the means."

"You got a way of twisting words, Kane. If I can't get cash from you, cash what's owed to me, I reckon I'll have to take it out in hide."

Kane braced himself as Quist drew himself up to full height, thrust his jaw forward in a belligerent manner and glared at Jock.

"Come on, Lou," Chad said. "We don't need no trouble here. Just forget it. At least for now."

"I don't forget," Quist said. He began to crouch, his muscles balling up like a snake coiling to strike.

"You can't get blood out of a turnip," one of the other hands said. "If Jock ain't got no money, Lou, what's the damned point?"

"Shut up, Fred," Quist said. The man who had spoken was Fred Naylor. Jock knew him, but they weren't friends.

"Lou, back down," Chad said. "You and Jock can talk it out later. Let the man eat his supper."

"You got the boss sticking up for you, Kane? Maybe you'd like to hide behind his chaps."

"Quist," Jock said, his voice measured and slow, "you blow real hard, but all I hear out of you is a little squeak."

Quist uncoiled and struck.

He threw a roundhouse right at Jock as if he were swinging a sledgehammer. Jock brought up his left arm and took the blow, but he staggered backward from the force of it. Quist followed up with a left jab that caught Jock on the tip of his chin.

Jock's head exploded. Lights danced in his brain as if they were inside his eyes. He tried to brace himself to deliver a blow of his own, but Quist charged him, head down, like a bull on the rampage. Quist head-butted Jock in the gut, knocking all the wind out of Jock's lungs.

Jock groaned and doubled over. Quist brought a fist down hard and slammed Jock in the back of the neck, knocking him to the ground.

The men watching, excited now, began to yell and encourage one or the other of the two combatants.

"Get him, Jock. Get up."

"You got him, Lou. Pour it on."

Quist didn't pounce on Jock when he was down. Instead, he drew back a leg and drove a boot hard into Jock's side. Jock rolled over, grabbed Quist's boot and twisted, throwing Quist off balance. Jock gave a hard wrench and Quist howled in pain as he cartwheeled to the ground, landing on his shoulder. The onlookers gave out a great cheer and Jock scrambled quickly to his feet. He was panting, and so was Quist, who was hurt in two places, his shoulder and his leg.

Jock grabbed Quist by the collar and jerked him backward. Then he drove a fist straight down into Quist's nose. The man yelled out in pain as his nose compressed and began squirting blood. He struggled to regain his footing and Jock followed up with another blow to Quist's left temple. Quist grunted and sprawled out on the ground. But his eyes flared with anger and cunning. He hauled off with a right hand and drove a fist into Jock's midsection once again.

Jock waddled backward, holding onto his footing through sheer willpower.

In a split second, Quist rose to his feet and waded into Jock, fists flying, arms flailing like erratic windmills. He struck Jock in the soft flesh of his side with punishing blows. Jock backpedaled to avoid the flurry of fists and parried the next two blows.

Jock twisted to one side as Quist continued his bullish charge, then knocked Quist's hat off and grabbed a hank of hair. He pulled hard and Quist's neck swung around in a half arc, until he was looking into Jock's eyes. Jock smashed Quist with a pile-driving right, felling him like an ox. Then Jock kicked Quist square in the belly, knocking the wind out of him until Quist's lips turned blue as he struggled to suck in air.

"Kill him, Jock," someone yelled.

"Finish him off, Kane."

"Come on, Lou, don't give up," hollered another.

Jock was oblivious to the shouts, hearing only the loud sound of his own breath and the pumping of his heart. His legs were wobbly, quivering, yet his whole body seemed charged with electricity. He was running on that force that floods a man's veins when he's in danger, when he's fighting for his life.

Quist was tough, but he was just stupid enough to make mistakes in a knockdown, drag-out fight such as this. Jock had had enough of it, though. The fight was senseless and should never have happened. He blamed himself, partly, for even talking to Quist. When a man was hot under the collar, it was best to walk away.

Jock stepped up and cocked his arm. He threw the punch with all his might and felt the shock of the blow shoot up his arm, making his senses scream with pain. He had driven his fist to the point of Quist's jaw and heard something crack. Whether it was his own knuckles breaking, Quist's neck, or his chin, Jock did not know. He saw Quist's eyes roll back in their sockets and then come back to their original positions, but horribly out of focus. Then Quist slumped over, his throat wheezing like a blacksmith's bellows. He went limp and stretched out, knocked cold by Jock's hammering fist.

"He's done for," a man said.

Jock let out a sigh.

"One of you boys get some water," Chad said. "Splash it on him."

Jock stood there, heaving for breath. A man stepped up behind him, put a hand on his shoulder. "Quist wasn't really mad at you, Jock, so much as at your brother Abel. You were just the handiest."

Jock turned around, bewildered, and looked into the eyes of Earl Foster, a man who once worked for him.

"We'd all like a piece of Abel right now," Foster said, and his eyes glinted with a flashing anger that made Jock wince. He could almost feel the heat from those burning, angry eyes.

Chapter 4

Jock stared at Earl Foster, completely bewildered by what he had said.

"What's Abel done to you, Earl? And to Quist, for that matter?"

Foster didn't say anything, just stared at Jock and shook his head.

"Jock," Chad said, "let it go for now. There's been enough bad blood spilled here. Take your plate and let's eat and let tempers cool."

Chad handed Jock his plate of food, growing cold now, and Jock took it as Foster walked away. He heard Quist spluttering as a man splashed a bucket of cold water over his face, drenching his shirt and trousers.

"It's all over with, Lou," Foster said.

"Maybe Jubilee will give you some hot grub to take your mind off Jock and his brother."

Quist groaned, unable to speak. He felt his jaw and nearly doubled up with the pain.

Chad led Jock away from the others and took him around behind the chuck wagon. Jock was aware of the murderous glances the other men shot at him as he passed them by. Jubilee was the only one who smiled, as if to reassure him that at least he was on Jock's side.

Chad sat down, leaning against one wagon wheel. Jock leaned against the other. He was still shaking, but a bite of food seemed to calm him, taking his mind off the bruises he had suffered during the fight. A man came around the tailgate of the wagon, carrying Jock's gunbelt.

"I hope you don't need this, but I'm plumb tired of carrying it," the man said.

"Jock, this is Dewey Ringler. He worked for Charlie Goodnight."

"Thanks, Dewey," Jock said, taking the gunbelt. "I hope I don't have to use that hogleg for anything more than killing rattlesnakes."

"Kane, you got one enemy in this outfit already. Lou Quist. Me, I'm on the fence. But Charlie told me once't that you was a good man. I hope like hell he was right."

"Charlie's a good judge of character," Chad said in Jock's defense. "But I'll vouch for Jock Kane any day of the week."

"That's good enough for me," Ringler said, and then turned on his heel and left Chad and Jock to their supper.

"What was that about my brother, Abel?" Jock asked, after Ringler was out of earshot. "I thought you said he borrowed money and then rode on."

"I might have made a big mistake there with Abel, Jock."

"How so?"

"I tried to hire him and his two friends for the drive to Ellsworth. Told him my plan, said I wanted you for my trail boss. He said he'd let me know. He came back two days later and paid me back the money he owed me. He was by himself."

"And?"

"I asked him where his two friends were and he said they'd hired on with the Cross J outfit."

"Damn," Jock said, chewing on a piece of meat, tucking it to one side of his mouth.

"Yeah, I thought the same thing. A couple of bad boys going even badder."

"What about Abel? Did he turn you down for the job with your outfit?"

"He said he was riding for the Cross J, too, and that they were heading out for Ellsworth themselves pretty quick. That was a week ago. I've got a scout over at the Cross J, two of 'em, really, who keep me informed about their plans to beat me to Ellsworth."

"Are you saying there's a chance the Cross J will cut you out of a sale up there in Kansas?"

"I am."

"That bastard," Jock said.

He was thinking of Curt Torgerson, the big Swede who owned the Cross J, a dirty-dealing Yankee who had come to Texas after the war and grabbed up land for taxes as an official with the federal government.

"Torgerson was born a bastard," Chad said, "and remains one to this very day."

Jock finished the stew and mopped up the gravy with a wedge of hardtack, his thoughts racing beyond that paling afternoon when long shadows began to stretch across the land, leaning away from the coming sunset.

"I can't figure why my brother would throw in with a rascal like Torgerson," Jock said finally. "To get back at me, maybe."

"He knew that you and Torgerson had a run-in?"

"Why, sure he did. I'd still be ranching next to your spread if Torgerson hadn't taken it away from our folks. In a way, he caused my mother's death, and maybe my father's, too. He broke their hearts when he showed them the papers and told them they had to get off their land. Land they had wrested from the Spaniards, the Mexicans, the Apaches, and who knows what all. Daddy had a small piece of land near Del Rio and we went there. At least it was paid for and the damned carpetbaggers couldn't grab it."

"I hated to see you leave, Jock. But you did well. You increased your holdings and all."

Jock set his plate down beside him and pulled out the makings. He offered the sack of tobacco to Chad, who shook his head. Jock built a quirly, lit it as the sun sank lower in the sky and the talk of the men became first a murmur, then a sporadic series of grunts. He could hear Jubilee scraping plates with dirt, banging them together, and his helper putting them into a gunnysack to take to the creek. Mac came by and got their plates, scraped them quickly with a knife, then put them into the sack he was carrying. The young man walked off toward the creek, his sack rattling softly despite his attempts to keep the plates from banging together.

"I've told Mac how easy it is to start a stampede," Chad said.

"If he drops that sack, that could do the trick," Jock said.

"Back to what we were talking about, Jock," Chad prompted when it turned quiet once again. "About your ranch over yonder in Del Rio."

"I was doing just fine until I made that drive to Abilene."

"What happened to you, Jock, could have happened to anybody. Nobody blames you."

"Abel blames me, and now it seems Quist bears me a grudge."

"Quist will get over it."

"I don't think so." Jock flexed his fingers, his sore knuckles, looked at them as if they belonged to someone else. They were scuffed and scratched, showing little lines of red where he had bled some. His other bruises throbbed, but he knew they were already beginning to heal.

"You still have your land, don't you, Jock?"

Jock laughed dryly. "A whole lot of empty land. It will take years for me to build another herd. I've got a few bulls and a handful of cows. It's getting harder and harder to find wild longhorns over Del Rio way, and harder still to round them up in Mexico and drive 'em over the Rio Grande."

"Yeah, I know what you mean," Chad said. "I finally had to hire Mexicans to round up cattle down in Mexico, and then pay them so much a head. I'll still come out all right if I can get this herd up to Ellsworth. Before Torgerson does, that is."

"How many head is Torgerson driving up?" Jock asked.

"I don't know. Nothing the size of my herd, though. And probably a lot of those he's herding are stolen. Torgerson is not averse to using a running iron, I know."

"Yeah. He got caught once. I don't know what happened though. He didn't get hanged and he didn't go to jail."

"You know why?"

Jock shook his head. The sun was very low on the western horizon by now and a breeze was making the end of his cigarette glow. But at least it took the smoke away from his eyes.

"The complainant—that's what the Texas Rangers called the man who had his cattle stolen—wound up dead."

"Dead? You mean murdered."

"Broken neck. Murder was never proved."

"Very convenient," Jock said.

"Jock, I've got a very good reason to ask you to boss my herd up to Ellsworth. I didn't want to tell you all this, but maybe what I say will change your mind."

"I doubt it. I'm still real shaky about running a herd that far. Especially one the size of yours. I just don't want the responsibility."

"What if you had another herd of your own, Jock? You'd have to drive it to the railhead to make any gain. Otherwise, you'd just have a lot of beef to husband and real empty pockets."

"Well, yeah, Chad. But that's not likely to happen any time soon."

Chad got up and stretched his legs. Jock could hear his knees creak. They were both getting toward that age when they could hear their own bones jar against one another when they stiffened up. And they stiffened up more often than not if they sat for a spell.

Jock put out his cigarette, which had burned down to a scrap. He got up, too, and looked to the west, where the sun burned acid rims to the clouds, turning white fluff into bronze and silver and gold. He didn't see Chad take a small bottle from his pocket and quickly take a sip. Chad shuddered as he put the bottle back, his face white as cuttlebone.

"Listen to this, Jock," Chad said. "Nobody

wanted to make this drive after what happened to you. Most of the hands are greenhorns. I had to put my ranch up to borrow enough money to pay my drovers and wranglers every month. If I don't make this drive, I'm wiped out. Worse than you."

"Maybe you should cut the size of the herd," Jock said.

Chad shook his head.

"I borrowed real heavy," he said. "And my buyer wants that many head. If you hire on, I'll pay you a hundred and fifty a month and found. I'm paying the hands thirty."

"That's a good offer, Chad. But, no."

Chad bit down and bunched his lips.

"Damn it, Jock, you're the only one I can depend on. You carry a lot of respect around here, despite what happened to you. You know how to handle men better than I do. You proved that in the army and since then."

"I don't want the job, Chad."

"I'm going to sweeten the offer, Jock. That's how bad I need you."

"Don't waste it on me, Chad. My mind is made up."

Jock started to walk away. Chad grabbed him by the elbow and pulled him back.

"Damn you, Jock, just listen, will you?"

"Chad, take your damned hand off my

arm." Jock's voice was as cold and hard as steel.

Chad dropped his hand as if it had been burned. "I'm sorry," he said. "I just didn't want you to leave before hearing the rest of what I have to say. I admit I'm desperate. Everything I own or give a damn about is riding on this single drive up north."

"Chad, that was the same situation I was facing when I took those three thousand head up to Abilene. Maybe I pushed too hard. Maybe I expected too much. Maybe I was wrong to go when I did."

"You couldn't help what happened, Jock. Mother Nature played her part, you know."

"The only thing is, Mother Nature's not accountable. She can take the blame but it costs her nothing. I lost everything I owned, just like that." Jock snapped his fingers. "One night of hail finished me off. I've gone over that night a thousand times in my mind. I still come up the same way. A loser."

"All right, Jock. This is the last time I'm going to ask you to trail boss my herd. I'll lay it all out for you. You can take it or leave it. I won't press you and I won't argue and I won't beg. One roll of the dice. Okay?"

Jock didn't answer right away. Instead, he pulled out the makings and began building a cigarette. It was a habit he had that unnerved some people, puzzled others. But it was his way of putting some distance between himself and an adversary who might be hotheaded. Chad was neither of these, but Jock knew they both had to be prepared for that last roll of the dice.

Maybe both of their lives depended on it. Maybe both their fates were in jeopardy.

Jock rolled a cigarette.

And he took his own sweet, slow time.

Chapter 5

Chad waited until Jock had finished rolling his cigarette. Then he pulled out a match and lit it for his friend.

"Are you ready to listen now, Jock?"

"I'm as ready as I'll ever be, I guess. Give it your best shot."

Chad didn't laugh. "All right. I offered you five times the pay I'm giving my hands. But this drive is so important to me, and you're so important to me, I'm willing to offer you ten percent of what we get for the herd in Ellsworth. That's forty dollars a head, son, and that should be right around what you would have gotten for your cattle if you'd made it through to Abilene."

"What would have been, what might have

been," Jock said, musing as he mulled over Chad's generous offer.

Chad said nothing, allowing his friend to ruminate in silence.

Jock watched a small band of longhorns grazing several hundred yards away, their calico hides shimmering in the sun, their legs moving woodenly whenever they moved, their horns casting off glints of light as they swung their heads or lifted them in wary vigilance.

He had no money. He had no future. He had no cattle. Not anymore. Chad was giving him a chance to populate his ranch with cattle like those he saw grazing, grazing as if they were waiting for something. Or someone.

"Fifteen thousand head," Jock said.

"Uh-huh."

"It's a hell of a responsibility."

"Yeah, it is."

"The men have to be good. And careful."

"Like you, Jock."

"There might be some weeding out."

"Might be."

"They'd all have to follow orders."

"Sure."

"First three days on the trail," Jock said.

"Stampedes?"

"Yeah. That's when they want to bolt back

for the home range. It could be one hell of a mess."

"That happen to you?"

"Yeah, it did," Jock said. "I broke them up after that. Into bunches we could handle better."

The memories of that drive unfurled in Jock's mind until he could see it all—the wide, well-marked trail churned up by thousands of cattle that had preceded them, the country sprawled in all directions like some living map where grasses grew and creeks ran like the veins of a living thing, and the land breathed and wafted up its scents until a man's head was full of perfume and the poignant aromas of dung and the sweat of animals and men. He had become drunk on it, and mindless of the dangers ahead, despite the early stampedes and the meanness of longhorns and the short patience of men on horseback. The giddiness of it all came back to him then, and he felt his resolve weaken and dissipate like the morning dew on cactus flowers when the rising sun warmed the day and streamed light into a man's heart.

"I'll take your herd up, Chad," Jock said finally, dreamy shadows flitting in his eyes as if he had returned from a state of rapture.

"We have to move them by tomorrow. Grass is about played out."

"I'll meet with the men, all of them, right at dawn. You have the remuda and the wranglers there, too. I want to look at this herd and, tomorrow, the horses. And tell every man to bring pistol and rifle. No exceptions."

"I'll spread the word, Jock," Chad said, beaming, his face bright as a white cloud sprayed with the last rays of the sun.

The two men shook hands.

"Go on then, Chad. I want to ride through the herd. Where do we bunk tonight?"

"We can ride back to the house, or we can bunk out here on the ground."

"Might as well get used to it," Jock said. "That's what bedrolls are for."

Chad laughed.

Jock caught up his horse, ignoring the stark glances of the men still hanging around the chuck wagon, smoking and talking in low tones.

"You goin' to ramrod this outfit, Kane?" one of the men said. His name was Burt Stubbins—Jock knew him.

"Any objections, Burt?"

"I ain't got none."

Jock mounted his horse and turned to the men.

"Anybody who doesn't want to ride with

me tomorrow can pack it in tonight. I mean to put you boys through hell and high water."

Somebody cursed.

Jock spat out his cigarette and turned his horse. Behind him, he could hear the low rumble of talk in his wake, and it didn't bother him at all. He knew how hungry the men were. They were almost as hungry as he was.

Chapter 6

Jock caught only fragments of the conversation that rose up behind him as he rode off into the sea of longhorns.

"Burt, you better watch what you say to Kane. Look what that bastard did to Lou."

"He got lucky," Quist said. "There'll be another time."

". . . ain't so tough . . ."

". . . he don't have eyes in the back of his head . . ."

Jock couldn't recognize the last two voices and they faded out. It didn't matter. He had enemies, new and old, in Chad's camp, and he'd have to deal with them when the time came.

For now, he was glad to get away by himself and see what kind of animals he'd be driving north. He almost couldn't believe he'd agreed to take on the job of trail boss for Chad Becker, but he'd given his word and shook hands on it, so this was his bed to lie on, good or bad.

Some of the longhorns eyed him as he passed, and others pawed the ground and took fighting stances as if ready to do battle. He recognized these as wild cattle. He would have to pick out a lead steer come morning, and hope the drovers could make a tame crowd out of these unruly and unpredictable beasts.

They were good cattle, all of them, and when he saw men riding herd, he waved to them from a distance. Some even waved back, but he wondered if they knew who he was, or if they were just acknowledging his wave in some kind of reflexive action. Some, he thought, were just glad to see another rider, for they were isolated and nervous, the way many men were before a big cattle drive. He wondered if they knew what they were in for, or if they just couldn't see that far ahead. It was one thing to watch over a herd on a pasture, quite another to handle a large bunch that had no taste for leaving home grass and venturing into unknown territory.

The burnished gold rim of the sun hung on

the horizon for a long spell, it seemed, the clouds hovering like smeared paints on a palette. The land itself glowed with the sunset, and the cattle seemed content to graze and let the horseman pass by without so much as a bellow or snort.

Ahead, well away from the fringes of the large herd gathered in that place, Jock saw three riders in a group, all staring to the northwest. So absorbed were they in something that they didn't notice Jock as he rode up behind them. Two had rifles out of their scabbards as if they were tracking game.

"Hello," Jock called when he was within earshot.

The riders all jerked around to look at him and Jock waved in a friendly manner just in case they were in a shooting mood.

"Riding up," Jock shouted. "Don't shoot."

One of the men laughed. It was a nervous laugh.

"Who are you?" one of the men asked.

"Jock Kane."

"Kane? I've heard that name before."

"What're you watching?" Jock asked. "Coyote?"

Two of the men were Mexicans. The one who had been speaking was a cowhand named Amos Beeson. He introduced himself quickly, after sheathing his Sharps carbine. "This here is Manuel Rivera, and this is Gilberto Fuentes."

Jock shook hands with all three men. Fuentes reluctantly put away his rifle, an old Enfield with a weathered stock and army sights, which he collapsed before slipping the weapon into its scabbard.

"No coyote, Mr. Kane," Beeson said.

"It was an Apache," Rivera said. "I seen him sneaking around the herd."

"It was an Apache, all right," Beeson said. "Up to no good. He saw us and snuck off. But he was marking the herd."

Jock's scalp prickled as if a clutch of baby spiders had just been hatched in his hair and were crawling through the strands. There was no such thing as one Apache. If these men saw one, that Indian was part of a band. There were not supposed to be any Apaches in this part of Texas, but everyone knew there were some who would never give up, who would never leave Texas and live on a reservation, or take to farming or live in town.

"Any word of Apaches hereabouts?" Jock asked.

"Oh, they's some," Beeson said. "Ever' so often they'll rustle a few head, then disappear until they get hungry, or broke, again."

The two Mexicans nodded in agreement.

"You weren't going to shoot him, were you, Beeson?"

"I thought about it."

The sun slipped down below the horizon, leaving just a small rim of shining gold, shimmering like some alchemist's molten disk on the far edge of the world. Jock looked over the three men, assessing them, not by the clothes they wore—mostly homespun—but by the way they sat their horses and the look in their eyes. Their features stood out, lit by the last rays of sunlight, and they seemed etched of hard stuff; the faces of men born to the land.

"I hope you didn't think about it too much," Jock said.

"What do you mean?" Beeson said.

"This the front of the herd?" Jock asked.

"Yeah, we're right at the head of it. The rest are back where you rode from."

"See any likely lead steers in this bunch?" Jock pulled out the makings and offered the sack around. The men shook their heads, still regarding him as an uninvited stranger, perhaps an enemy, suddenly intruding on them as if he had some stake in what they were about with the cattle.

"Naw, I ain't been lookin'," Beeson said,

meaning it was none of Jock's business right then.

"Well, this herd's going to be moving north tomorrow," Jock said. "If you had fired off that Sharps of yours, we might have to chase down a lead steer in the dark."

"Say, mister, who in hell are you?" Beeson asked point-blank.

"I told you my name."

"Yeah, I got that. Didn't you lose a whole herd up in Kansas a while back?"

"I didn't lose them," Jock said. "They all got killed in a hailstorm."

"Yeah, that's what I mean. What business you got here?"

"Becker sent for me. He wants me to trail boss this herd up to Ellsworth."

"Huh?" Beeson looked at Kane as one would look at a bald-faced liar. "You, the trail boss?"

One of the Mexicans swore under his breath, in Spanish. It was a mild curse and mentioned a cockroach and ancestry.

Jock finished rolling his cigarette, licked it and stuck it in his mouth. He struck a match and lit the cigarette, then left it to dangle from his lips.

"That's right," Jock said. "We'll have a meeting tomorrow morning and I'll lay it all out for you. If you're signed on, that is."

"Oh, we're signed on," Beeson said. "But I got to question Mr. Becker's sanity about hiring you on as trail boss after what happened to you up in Kansas."

"I'm sure a lot of people will question his sanity before this is over. And they might question mine, and yours, for that matter."

"I got to think real hard about this, mister."

"Well, you got all night, Beeson. Think as hard as you want. I'm going to look at those steers up at the head of the herd. You boys keep a sharp eye out in case that Apache shows up."

"What are we supposed to do if he does?" Beeson asked.

"Well, don't shoot him unless you want to chase cows all night. Rope him."

"Rope him?"

Jock didn't answer. He rode off with a smile breaking on his lips. He heard the Mexicans conversing in Spanish, and his grin widened.

He understood every word in their language.

They were saying that he was one crazy gringo and they hoped that Apaches took his scalp.

Jock felt good about meeting those men, regardless of their feelings about him.

It was a start.

Chapter 7

The sun slid below the horizon as Jock rode across the front of the herd. This was the leading edge, he knew, and somewhere in the bunch was his herd leader. There was still plenty of light to see by, and as he rode close to the cattle, he watched like a man at an auction. Some of the steers and cows continued grazing, paying him no mind. Others looked at him disconsolately, lifting their heads for a moment, then bending them back down as if he were of no consequence.

After riding across in front of the cattle, Jock turned his horse and headed back the way he had come. He had seen some promising candidates and when he found them again, he turned his horse north. One cow left the herd and followed him. She was big and had fire in her eyes. He reined his horse to a stop abruptly and turned to face the cow that had followed him.

She swung her head and pawed the ground, glaring at him. Challenging him. She bore scars on her face and neck, and her left shoulder was veined with an old wound that had turned black and hairless, as if she had been gouged deeply and a worm had replaced the flesh and become petrified. When she moved her leg, the dead worm undulated and corkscrewed as if it were somehow alive.

"Well, hello there, gal," Jock said, his voice low and his tone soothing.

The cow lifted her head and mooed.

Her hide was a patchwork of brindle and cream, her boss thick and heavy, her horns not as large as some of the steers, but formidable enough, he decided. He turned his horse and spurred it to trot away. The cow followed, believing, he thought, that it was responsible for the horse's retreat. Jock stopped and the cow stopped, too, and pawed the ground, lowing softly as if in warning.

Good, Jock thought. She was territorial. She was protecting her place in the herd. There was a term for it that he had heard the Mexicans use when talking about bullfighting. *Querencia.* When a matador worked the bull—

caping it, testing it, preparing it for the final moment, the kill—the bull would always find a place to make a last stand. This the Spanish called *querencia*, the place the bull preferred. Home ground. The word meant "preference," he thought. This cow he faced could lead a large herd; she could make the others follow because she had that possessiveness of the ground she either stood or walked on without fear.

"You'll do, lady," he said. "What should I call you? You, with that calico hide. How about Calico Sal? That good enough for you?"

The cow eyed him, as if listening to the sound of his voice.

He and the cow would never be friends, he knew, but he would pick her to lead the herd to Kansas.

"Beeson," Jock called. "Come on over, will you?"

The Mexicans had gone back to tending the herd and Beeson was nearby. He rode over.

"What you got?" Beeson asked.

"See that cow there?" Jock pointed at Calico Sal.

"Hard to miss."

"I think she's going to be my lead cow tomorrow. Keep an eye on her, will you?"

"She's young and probably pregnant," Beeson said.

"That's fine. I'm calling her Calico Sal."

"I never heard of naming a cow, less'n it was a milk cow. This'n ain't that. She's as wild as they come."

"You treat this cow as if she were a queen, Beeson, you hear me?"

"Well, I don't know. Mr. Becker ain't said nothing to me about you being ramrod of this outfit. And, until I hear . . ."

Jock cut him off.

"Beeson, let's get something straight. Either you take my word and follow my orders right now, or ride on back to the chuck wagon and draw your pay."

Beeson swallowed what might have been a lump in his throat, but might also have been air, or something imagined. Whatever it was, stuck there, and he struggled to get a gulp of oxygen past it and into his lungs. He looked intently at Jock as if trying to read what was in his eyes, as if doubting what his ears had just heard. It was a long moment of doubt, and an even longer moment of pondering a decision he must make.

Jock waited him out, his gaze steady, hard as black agate.

"I reckon I can do what you ask for a night, Kane. I can always see Mr. Becker tomorrow and see what he has to say about you."

"Fair enough," Jock said. "I'm obliged."

As Jock rode off, Beeson watched him, a puzzled look on his face. He lifted his hat and scratched the back of his head as if that would settle some of his doubts about the stranger named Jock Kane.

The shadows began to coalesce, and the clouds in the west turned to ashes as their colors faded. Jock rode along the edge of the herd, back toward the chuck wagon, gliding through shadows that had puddled up beneath his horse's hooves, and then he and the horse were shadows and the dark came on. The stars began to wink on, one by one, like the distant lights of towns.

Self-doubt began to inch into Jock's thoughts. He had finished the easy part, picking out a lead cow for the long drive north. Tomorrow he would have to face the drovers and wranglers who would be tending the large herd. He would have to establish himself as their leader, and with his history he knew it would not be easy. By now, the word would be spreading that he was taking over as trail boss for Chad Becker. That would stick in the craws of some of the men. Others might take him at face value, or give him a chance to prove himself. Still others might give him the benefit of the doubt, knowing that the herd would move slowly and that they could always quit if he didn't prove out.

Jock knew what he had to do. As soon as he finished addressing the men, he'd have to put them to work, scatter them so that they couldn't grumble or gripe before putting spur to horse, and begin driving the herd. If he could get through that first day, he might have a chance to win the doubters over. If he could make allies of them, their voices could drown out those of the protesters.

Lou Quist would be his first problem, but he knew there would be others. He had bested Quist in the first encounter, or at least brought the fight to a draw. It wouldn't always be so easy, he knew, and he hoped it didn't reach the point of gunplay.

As Jock approached the wagon, he encountered a lone man some distance from the campfire. He was smoking a pipe and gazing up at the stars.

"Howdy," Jock said, pulling on the reins to bring his horse to a stop. "Nice evening."

"Um, yeah. Nice enough."

"I'm Jock Kane."

"I know who you are."

"May I ask who you are?"

"Name's Dewey Ringler, for what it's

worth. I'm the one who held your gunbelt when you tangled with Lou Quist."

"That's right. I hope to learn the names of all the drovers as quick as I can."

"I ain't no drover. I'm a horse wrangler."

"Sorry. My mistake."

"Maybe that ain't your only mistake, Kane."

"What do you mean, Ringler?"

"Nothing. I was just thinking out loud."

"No harm in that, I reckon," Jock said.

"You might hear a lot of that, come morning."

"What, thinking out loud?"

"Men speaking their minds," Ringler said.

"No harm in that either."

"Well, you'll have a lot of eyes on you, Kane. You got a reputation."

"I imagine we all do, to some extent."

"Yep, that's what a man is: his reputation."

"Men change. Reputations change."

Ringler snorted. "Not that much," he said. "A leopard don't change its spots."

"I'd like a chance, at least," Jock said.

"You'll get your chance, Kane. These are all good boys. But they can measure a man, just the same."

"A chance is all I ask." Jock drew in a

breath, then touched a finger to his hat brim. "Well, good night, Ringler. Nice talking to you."

"Just watch your back, Kane. That's my advice."

"Thanks."

Jock rode on to the edge of the light around the campfire. Men were sitting around it, but not close. They weren't cold; they just wanted to be able to see each other in the darkness before they turned in or took their turns as nighthawks tending to the herd.

Ringler's words echoed in his mind.

"Watch your back."

That was a fair warning, he supposed. The lines were drawn.

Now it was up to him to get the herd to Ellsworth with as little trouble as possible.

But Jock knew it would not be easy.

He had enemies in camp. And, probably, some of them were sitting around the campfire at that very moment.

Well, they would have to live with it, and so would he.

Chapter 8

Curt Torgerson had already begun to move his herd north. He knew that Chad Becker was due to head out at any time and he wanted to beat the man to Ellsworth. He had better than six thousand head bearing the Cross J brand, most of them protesting as they left their home range after dark. But the rancher knew he had to beat Becker to market at the railhead if he were to realize a profit.

"Where in hell is Dub?" Torgerson asked, looking back through the darkness.

"He'll be along, boss," Rafe Castle said. "You know he's got to be mighty careful."

"I need to know what Becker's up to, when he plans to move out."

Both men were riding drag, mainly because Torgerson was waiting for his man, Dub Morley, to report to him from inside the Becker camp. He was paying the man enough money to be his spy, and he hadn't heard from him in two days.

"Well, you know we got a head start on Becker. He's got cattle strung out for miles. Far as we know, he still don't have no trail boss."

Torgerson patted the withers of the palomino he rode, a horse whose color matched his own hair. He did this more to reassure himself than the horse, for he was worried. Dub knew they were moving out—had known it for a week. And Dub knew that he was to give a report on Becker's progress before Torgerson's herd headed north.

He had long been envious of Becker's spread, and when he heard that Chad was going to run such a large herd up to Ellsworth, it had galled him. He had vowed to beat Chad to the punch. Torgerson's cows would have first crack at the grass along the trail, grow fat and leave Becker's cattle to forage in ever-widening swaths, slowing him down, making him miss out on his big sale.

Becker had beaten him in a land dispute some years back and Torgerson had never forgotten it. This drive was not only his way of getting revenge, but of making enough money to enlarge his own holdings and make him a richer man than Becker. Torgerson wanted the last laugh.

"Listen," Rafe said a few moments later, breaking into Torgerson's thoughts. "I think someone's coming up from the south."

Torgerson straightened up in the saddle and turned his head. He cupped a hand behind his right ear.

"Yah, I hear him. Must be Dub."

"He's wearing out leather."

The stars burned a diamond light through the haze of dust churned up by the cattle, and the close air was filled with the acrid ammonia smell of urine and the pungent aroma of cow shit plopped across the plain. Torgerson reined his horse to a halt and turned it so that he could see the rider when he emerged from the darkness.

Dub rode up a few seconds later on a grullo. He saw Rafe and Curt, and slowed to a trot.

"That you, Curt?" Dub called out.

"Me'n Rafe, Dub. What you got for me?"

"Ooowee. Boss, am I glad to see you. Didn't know you was this far north."

"I told you we were moving out tonight."

"I got here quick as I could. Hard to sneak off. But I drew the first watch."

Dub was panting, and his horse was blowing from the fast ride. Rafe kept looking over his shoulder at the retreating herd, as if measuring the distance they'd have to ride to catch up to it.

"So, what's the story?" Torgerson asked.

"Plenty, boss. But you ain't going to believe none of it. Becker's done hired Jock Kane as trail boss. Don't that beat all?"

Torgerson reared back in his saddle, stunned. "Jock Kane? Are you sure?"

"Yep," Dub said. "And Kane's going to head out tomorrow at first light."

Rafe swore under his breath. Torgerson just sucked in air, as if he had been dealt a fistblow to the gut.

"Well, maybe that ain't so bad," Dub said. "Don't ya know? Some is grumbling that Kane is a Jonah, pure bad luck on a cattle drive. Him and Quist got into it when Kane first rode in. Kane owes everybody and his brother for that last drive when he lost all three thousand head up in Kansas."

"That's true," Torgerson said. "Hiring Kane on might work to our advantage."

"Sure, boss," Rafe said. "Hell, I know men as would like to put his lights out over that drive. Not only Quist, but a dozen others."

"I wonder what Chad was thinking," Torgerson said. "I can't figure out why he'd hire someone like Jock Kane as a drover, much less a trail boss."

"They was friends," Dub said. "Fought together in the war. Second Texas, I think. They ranched together some before the war."

"Yeah, maybe that's it," Torgerson said. "Still, I think Becker's a fool to hire Kane on as trail boss."

"Maybe not," Rafe said. "Kane's a pretty tough old boy. How'd he do with Quist, Dub?"

"He put Quist down," Dub said.

Torgerson snorted. He didn't like any of it, and he was thinking. Thinking hard.

"Rafe, we might have us a problem here. We got Jock's brother hired on."

"Yeah, that's right," Rafe said.

"You better go fetch him, Rafe. I got to talk to that boy. Get something straight."

"Sure, boss. I know just where Abel be."

Rafe turned his horse and rode off toward the tail end of the herd. The herd was moving slowly, grazing, snatching at grass, grumbling with loud bawling when the drovers made them move.

"You better get on back, Dub. Before someone misses you."

"Oh, I took care of that, boss. I told my

nighthawk partner I was chasing strays. He was half asleep in the saddle. I think he got into the barleycorn."

"Drinking's not good on a drive," Torgerson said.

"Tell you the truth, I think Becker's been tippling."

"Becker? I never knew him to be fond of the bottle."

"Well, he's pulling on something that ain't water. From a little brown bottle. I seen him pull it out of his pocket a time or two when he thought nobody was looking. And a couple of times I seen him heaving after his supper and he don't eat breakfast. He just sucks on that bottle neck and then goes off by himself like he's got himself in a stupor."

"Be damned," Torgerson said.

"Almost forgot to tell you, boss. Some of the boys seen an Apache this evening."

"One Apache?"

"Just one."

Torgerson snorted. "What was he doing, this Apache?"

"Boys figure he was a scout. He run off and that was that."

"Where to? Where'd he run, Dub?"

"Off north. Toward where you was, I reckon."

"We didn't see nary."

"Well, where's they's one . . ." Dub said.

Torgerson thought about that part of Dub's report. Could be nothing. Or, could be they were in for trouble later on. Not at night. Never at night. But maybe, when they least expected it, some skulking Apaches would sneak up and cut out some of the herd—a few head, maybe—and run them off to their camp, or sell them for a few pennies a head, get enough to buy whiskey or bullets for their rifles. There were still Apaches round and about, he knew. Kiowas, too. And, Comanches. He'd see one or two every so often, way off in the distance, like coyotes, just skulking and watching and then disappearing into the haze of sun and dust, like ghosts or stray dogs.

He had never had any trouble with any of them. Not up close. Though some ranchers had. Mainly, the Apaches just looked and sometimes rustled a cow or two, then would not be seen again for long periods of time.

But now, Becker taking to the bottle—that was something to keep in mind. Maybe that's why he hired on Jock Kane. Chad was losing his grip on the old plow handle, slipping into the arms of John Barleycorn. Maybe his old lady had cut him off. Maybe that daughter of his was slipping the apron strings and taking some of the hands into the hayloft. All kinds of things could drive a man to drink, even a man like Chad Becker. It was something to think about all right. But it was Jock Kane who was the puzzle piece. Why would Becker hire on a man like that? As trail boss, no less? Yah, it was a big puzzle piece, that Kane, and might just work in his favor. A drunk rancher and a washed-up rancher with empty pockets. Yah, it just might work in his favor, Torgerson mused.

Rafe rode up then, another man following behind him—Abel Kane.

"Here he is, boss," Rafe said.

"Mr. Torgerson," Abel said. "You wanted to see me?"

"Yeah, I did, Kane. You doing all right with my cows?"

"Yes, sir. I like it just fine. Kind of strange running herd at night, though, what with the rattlers and the old prairie dog holes." Abel laughed self-consciously.

"I wanted to ask you a question, Kane. Did you know your brother was hired on by Chad Becker to drive his herd up to Ellsworth?"

Abel went quiet for a long moment. "No, sir, I reckon I didn't. I ain't seen Jock since I left Del Rio."

Abel was a pudgy man, taller, bigger, and

younger than his brother. He had sloping shoulders and peevish twitches at the corners of his small, feral eyes. His lips were as pudgy as he was, continually wet and pouting, like a baby's, or a woman's.

"I got to ask you something, Abel," Torgerson said. "And you think real hard before you answer."

"Yes, sir," Abel said.

"There could be trouble on this drive. We got two big herds competing for the same trail, heading for the same railhead. Your brother is heading one of them."

"Yes, sir, I reckon."

"If push came to shove and we got into a brouhaha with Becker's bunch, whose side would you be on?"

Abel didn't hesitate. "I ride for the brand, sir. I'd fight on the Cross J side."

"And, if your brother threw down on you, what would you do?"

"Why, I'd blow him to hell, boss."

Torgerson smiled. Even in the starlight, the men there could all see it.

"That's all I wanted to know, Abel. You can go on back now."

"Good night, boss," Abel said, a lilt to his voice that hadn't been there before.

"Good night, Abel," Torgerson said.

He watched Kane ride away and let out a long sigh. "Let's hope it doesn't come to that, Rafe. But I had to know. You keep an eye on him, hear?"

"Sure, boss. And them other two who came with him."

"Yeah, that's right. Let's see if birds of a feather really do flock together."

A few moments later, Dub rode back south, his job finished for the evening. Rafe and Torgerson caught up with the herd and breathed in the dust and the cattle smells, the stars overhead quivering in the dust cloud, shimmering like tiny candles at the bottom of a well.

Chapter 9

Long before dawn, the X8 herds, three separate bunches, set up a lowing that grew to a crescendo as the eastern sky turned ashen and a pale cream light seeped through the opening seam in the fabric of night. The night before, Jock had sent orders to the nighthawks to keep the herds bunched up so that by morning, their bellies rumbling with hunger, they would be ready to move on to new grass when the drovers headed them north.

He had also instructed the drovers to slip away from the herds at first light and gather at the chuck wagons. A second wagon had rumbled in during the night, loaded with supplies until its springs groaned under the strain.

Now Jock stood there by the fire, a cup of

steaming coffee in his hand, a cigarette dangling from his lips, watching the men stream into camp from all directions. Their faces were gaunt and drawn from sleepiness and weariness, their tempers seething just beneath the surface, their nerves jangling like the spurs they wore, knowing they would soon be moving the great herd into a single mass, heading toward the faint pole star—into the great unknown.

Chad sat nearby, holding his coffee cup close to his face, the steam rising to his nostrils in smoky tendrils, his eyes half closed and still gritty from the sandman's visit during the night. He, too, was drawn tight as a wet cinch, his stomach fluttering with a thousand wings.

Most of the men seemed tense, edgy, uneasy. That was the way it was before a drive, Jock knew. Especially a drive this big, with this many cattle. They all knew what could go wrong, or should know. But it wouldn't hurt to remind them a little before they started out.

Jubilee and Mac were making sandwiches for the boys to pack with them. There would be no breakfast this morning. Jock wanted them lean as whippets when they started out, hungry as hunters, so they'd be sharp, alert, this first day. But they would all have hard-tack and jerky to fill their roiling stomachs, something to chew on besides dust if they felt the hunger pangs begin to gnaw at their empty bellies.

The coffee would run right through them and they would all have a second good piss before they started out.

And still the men streamed in, out of the rising mists and fog of morning as the rent in the eastern sky widened and the cream spread, bringing light to things unseen and unidentifiable in the dark. The last star faded and the remnant of the moon was just a thin etching on frosted glass, a ghost left over from the night.

"Let me know when all the hands are in, Chad, will you?" Jock whispered to Becker.

"They're just about all here, I think. One or two more."

Chad didn't look well, Jock thought. He had seen him take a swallow of coffee, then walk away from the fire and the chuck wagon and heave his guts. When Chad returned he seemed all right, and sipped his coffee without losing it. Jock chalked it up to nerves. A man's stomach could quiver like a facial tic just before a big drive. Especially a man with Chad's responsibility. Some of the hands seemed pretty relaxed, probably because they didn't understand the full import of what they were to engage in sometime very soon.

Two more men rode in and Jubilee saw to it that they were given sandwiches wrapped in a thick, oily kind of brown paper. Jock didn't know that the cook smeared bacon fat on the paper before using it. It was one of Jubilee's many secrets.

"All here, Jocko," Chad said.

Jock finished his coffee and spit out some grounds that had passed his lips. He set his tin cup down and walked to the other side of the fire so that it blazed behind his back.

"Men," he began, "I'm Jock Kane and I've been hired as trail boss for this outfit. We've got a long, hard drive ahead of us, clear up to Ellsworth, Kansas. I can guarantee you'll want to quit more than once. But, if you make the whole drive, you'll know you've done something and nobody can ever take that away from you.

"Now," Jock continued, "some of those times will be during or after a stampede. And with this many cattle in a herd, there's a strong likelihood that something will spook one cow, or half a dozen, and set the whole bunch to running. Usually this happens in the first few days of a drive, and some say it's better to push the herd hard off of home ground so they don't get that notion in their heads.''

Some of the men laughed, and Jock paused.

''But I hold that we start out slow, get the herd used to being driven, let you boys make friends with some of the cows.''

More laughter from the group.

''So, we'll take it slow. Now, a lot of cows will want to turn back. Your job is to keep them moving north, no matter what.''

Jock paused, waiting for his words to sink in.

''Stampedes aren't the only thing we have to face. There might be Indians. In fact, I can almost guarantee that, too. And it's not only the hostiles we have to watch out for, but the friendlies, too. They'll want to steal our horses. So, I hope you wranglers will be well armed and on the lookout. As for the cows, friendlies will steal them and try to sell them back to you the next day. Hostiles will run them off and you won't ever see them again.

''Don't rile the farmers and ranchers we encounter along the way. If you get in trouble crossing a man's land, come and get me and I'll try and throw some oil on the troubled waters. Up in Kansas, it's a different story.

The farmers there are downright mean and devilish."

An uneasy murmur rose up from the assemblage.

"Up in Kansas," Jock continued, "they just flat don't like cattle mowing down their corn and gobbling up their wheat."

Laughter, again.

"The farmers up there will rag you and shoot at you and try to drive you off. I'll try and take care of those situations. Some of them will plow around their soddies and the law in Kansas says that's a fence. If you drive cattle across that plowed furrow, you can be arrested for trespassing. I had to bail out a hand or two when we ran into that kind of trouble."

Jock heard some of the men begin to grumble.

"All right," he said. "Don't look for trouble. I just want you to know some of the things that might happen on this drive. Let's get along with each other. Those of you who think I owe you money, I promise you this. When we get the herd up to the railhead and Chad pays us all off, I'll clean up those debts. I swear on it. Now, for this morning's work."

The men went silent, waiting for their immediate orders.

"We'll separate into three groups since we have three herds we're going to make into one. I'll ride up ahead of the main herd and scout ahead for both our noon stop and where we'll spend the night. I need a man in charge of each group."

The men all looked at each other and began talking about which should be in charge. Finally, one stepped out, then another, and still another. Jock nodded his approval.

The men were Earl Foster, who would drive the last herd into the main bunch; Burt Stubbins, who would take the second group; and Dewey Ringler, who would ride drag on the first herd. Fred Naylor would ride point. Jock knew him and picked him out of the crowd.

"Who's the head wrangler here?" Jock asked.

A man stepped forward.

"What's your name?" Jock asked.

"Jesus. Jesus Quintana."

" 'Sus," someone in the crowd said. The others all laughed.

" 'Sus, you'll bring the horses up after the last bunch is drove in."

"They call him Suzy Q," Chad said.

Jock smiled. "All right, Suzy Q. You got enough hands to help you?"

"Yes," Quintana said.

Jock then turned to Daggett, the cook.

"Jubilee, you bring the chuck wagons up to the head of the main herd with me. I'll give you some lead time to set up for supper. That all right with you?"

"That's fine," Daggett said.

"All right, then, head out. The rest of you," Jock said, "will come to the head of the herd for supper when we stop for the night. We won't stop at noon today. Let's try to get ten miles, but I'll settle for less, just so's we keep these cows heading north. So long and good luck."

Quist threw Jock a dirty look, but Jock ignored it. He saw that Lou went with the men heading out to bring in the last bunch.

"Well, we're ready, I guess," Chad said. "I think the men will work for you, Jocko."

"They'll work for themselves, I hope. I don't care if they like me or not. I want them to fall in love with these cows."

Chad laughed. Then he grimaced briefly as a spasm stiffened him, causing him to bend over slightly.

"Anything wrong?" Jock asked.

"Nope, just a twinge. The coffee maybe."

"Well, let's ride up to the head of this herd

and see if that lead cow I picked out last night is ready to take us up to Kansas.''

Chad's face drained of color, but he recovered quickly and walked to his horse, which was already saddled. Jock followed him, his eyes narrowed to slits.

They hadn't even started work yet and already he knew he had a problem. He was wondering if Chad was well enough to make the long drive to Ellsworth. He wouldn't make an issue of it now, but it was the beginning of a worry. He hoped that worry didn't get any bigger. He was not reassured when he saw Chad reach into his pocket and pull out a small bottle, uncork it and take a swallow.

Jock wondered what kind of medicine Chad was taking, and why. By the time he mounted up, Chad looked a lot better, with the color returned to his cheeks. They followed the two chuck wagons at a distance as the morning brightened, the sun already warming the land and burning off the dew and mist.

Jock breathed deeply of the fresh air and then dug in his pocket for his makings. He waved to the men he passed and some of them waved back. Jock hoped the day would be as good at the end as it was now, at the beginning.

Chapter 10

The day went to hell for Jock Kane.

And it didn't take long.

The drovers driving in the second large herd fought for every inch of ground. The lead steer kept turning back, while others bolted back to the home range. Finally, the herd scattered in all directions, breaking up like a covey of quail flushed from cover. The men chased, roped, bulldogged and hogtied the wilder ones, dragged them back into the gather until their horses, and they, were worn down to nubs.

Jock had to ride back to help sort it all out, and he designated a few hands to start milling the main body of the herd, then sent out drovers to round up the strays. He ordered some men to make a wide circle and drive back any cattle they encountered. It was a big job and it took hours to swell the herd back to something resembling its original size.

He had left Chad to scout ahead of the first herd, telling him to find a place to bed down the group that was far short of ten miles from their starting place. It was the best he could hope for, maybe five or six miles, giving him time to bring the other two herds in behind them into a single bunch.

Now Jock called over to the lead drover of the first herd, a man named Vic Cussler; a lean, rawboned man with a face leathered by the sun, the lines next to his eyes like thick, tough cords, his thin mouth a slit in his hatchet-chiseled face, aquiline nose broken in at least two places.

"Cussler, let's you and me pick out a lead steer that won't run back to home ground."

"Jeez, Kane, I thought I had me a good one picked out, horns as long as an oak limb, mean-eyed, slat-ribbed, long-legged sonofabitch."

"Well, your lead steer was the first to bolt, wasn't he?"

"Damn right. I'd like to kill that sonofabitch if I could ever find him."

"We won't be killing any cattle, Cussler.

Let's just find another one more willing to go to Kansas."

When they got the herd milling, Jock and Cussler rode slowly around the perimeter, both observing the behavior of those cattle nearest to them. Jock knew they couldn't cover the whole herd, but he hoped to find a lead steer in one of the milling bunches.

"What exactly are you looking for?" Cussler asked. "One with a lot of horn? Big-boned? A runner?"

"I'll see it in his eyes," Jock said. "Look over there. Look at the ones watching us. I'm hoping one will break and come out of the pack with fire in its eyes."

"Hell, a lot of them will do that, Mr. Kane."

"Call me Jock, will you? Mr. Kane was my father."

Cussler chuckled. "All right, Jock. I had what I thought was a good lead steer picked out. I don't know what happened."

"You probably did. Sometimes you don't get one the first day, or even the second. I think I found a good one last night, but I could be wrong. We'll know more tonight and even more in a couple of days, whether or not I chose the best lead cow."

They rode very slowly, both looking at

bunches of cows, and individuals. Some grumbled at their passing, letting out low timorous sounds, or snorting at them, pawing the ground. None of the cattle broke ranks, however.

Then, ahead of them, one of the steers trotted out of the pack. It didn't have the longest set of horns, nor was it as big as some of the other longhorns. But there was something about the way it stepped out that caught Jock's eye.

"Let's take a look at that one," he told Cussler.

"Looks right ordinary to me, Jock."

"We'll see. Look at the other cattle. They're watching him."

"Yeah, you're right. Some of them are a-looking at that one."

Jock reined up and yelled at the lone steer standing outside of the bunched herd. "Ho boy!"

The steer swung its head and looked at both men. Cussler had halted his horse, as well.

Jock reined his horse to the left, turning it, touched his spurs lightly to its flanks. The horse stepped out a few feet. The steer started to follow it. Other cattle in the herd pushed through the outer flanks and started to follow the lone steer. Jock reined up and the steer halted, glaring at horse and rider.

Jock repeated the action, making his horse travel a bit farther before reining it to a halt.

The steer followed Jock and several other cows separated from the herd and started to follow, also. Then the entire line of cows turned and fell into step.

Jock had his lead steer. He turned to Cussler and beckoned to him.

"You'll be all right now, Cussler?"

"Looks like it. Thanks. Say, I heard you and Quist got into it and you made him eat some dirt."

"My fist slipped," Jock said, a wry smile playing beneath the shadow of his cigarette.

"Yeah," Cussler said. "I wouldn't trust Quist as far as I could throw that steer there."

"Well, trust is a pretty big thing. I don't lay it on many men. Be seeing you, Cuss," Jock said, feeling a familiarity with the man now that they had found a lead steer together and the morning was smoothing out.

"Yep, Jock. You be careful, hear?"

Jock waved good-bye and set out to find the other herd that had turned back. When he did, they were already breaking from the milling circle and headed north in the wake of the first bunch. He rode to the head of the herd and ran into Dewey Ringler.

"I see you got yourself a leader," Jock said. "That old mossy-horned cow."

"Yeah. How's Cussler doing?" Ringler wore his hair short-cropped under a battered felt hat that had long since lost its original blocking. It wasn't a Stetson, but it did give his face some shade. Ringler had crackling blue eyes and a set of good teeth that he kept polished with cigarette ashes. He had a warm smile and seemed a friendly sort.

Jock stretched up from the stirrups and looked back over the herd that was untangling itself beneath a sea of horns.

"You got them moving, Dewey," Jock said.

"Yeah, but it's been a bitch willy of a morning, I'll tell you. We still got men rounding up strays. Some five, six miles away. These cows just don't want to go nowhere."

"Think you can handle it?" Jock asked.

"We may leave a few behind, but we got most of them. If they don't spook, we'll catch up to that front herd before nightfall."

"Before sunset, Dewey. I don't want to be chasing cows in the dark."

"Well, you're the boss. I just wish the cows knew that."

Jock laughed. At least Ringler had a sense of humor, dry as it was. Ringler never cracked a smile and Jock saw the sweat on him, soaking through his shirt and glistening on his forehead, slick as oil on his hands and forearms.

"And I want every stray picked up and returned to the herd," Jock said. "Got that?"

"Something you ought to know, Kane."

"Yeah?"

"Take a ride with me. I want to show you something."

Jock watched as Ringler looked around as if to get his bearings. Then the drover rode off to the south and west, his head bent, eyes scanning the ground. Ringler touched spurs to his horse's flanks and put the animal into a trot. He headed for a clump of prickly pear. When he reached it, he circled, then halted his horse. He swung out of the saddle and dropped his reins. Stooping over, he picked up something that was on the ground.

"What is that?" Jock asked as he rode over and looked down at the object in Ringler's hand.

Ringler handed a stick of milled wood up to Jock.

"I think we got us a traitor," Ringler said.

Jock turned the piece of wood over in his

hands. There was a large twenty-penny nail driven into one end, with blood on the tip.

"I chucked it over here after I found it," Ringler said. "These cattle didn't go to running on their own. Somebody made sure they spooked."

"I've never seen anything like this," Jock said.

"It's a kind of cattle prod," Ringler said. "Homemade."

"You mean . . . ?"

"I mean somebody rode through this herd early this morning, a-swinging that stick with the nail in it and set the cattle to running. It probably took only one cow to set the others off. Somebody wanted to hold us up."

"Who?"

Ringler shrugged. "I have no idea," he said. "I didn't see it happen, but one of the strays I rounded up near here had blood streaming from some holes in its hip. Flies were sucking on the blood. Whoever did it, drove that nail in pretty deep."

"Yeah," Jock said. He looked at the nail again, and touched a finger to the tip. It had been sharpened with a file and was very sharp.

"I heard a cow bawling its head off just before the herd bolted. I couldn't make out where it was and I didn't see nobody around. Next thing I knew, the whole bunch was scattering, running at top speed."

"I'll keep this," Jock said. "See if anyone else knows about it."

Ringler caught up his horse and climbed back in the saddle. He looked at Jock as he rode up.

"Kane, you probably won't ever find out who made this prod, but you got a rattlesnake riding to Kansas with us. This ain't all he's going to do."

"No, you're probably right," Jock said. "But I'll find out who's trying to hold us up. He'll give himself away, sooner or later. Meantime, you keep your eyes peeled. Let me know if any one of the hands in your bunch does something that doesn't look right. Rides off by himself or fools with the cattle, or comes up with another of these prods."

"I can't watch everybody and do my job," Ringler said.

"No. Just keep a lookout."

"I will." Ringler rode off to tend to the herd, leaving Jock to ride on ahead and scout.

Jock stuck the prod in his saddlebag, the smooth end jutting out. He didn't want anyone to see the nail until he was good and ready.

Meanwhile, he wondered if Chad knew that someone in his hire was working for Torgerson. For that was the only one Jock could think of who had something to gain by making sure Chad's cattle didn't reach Ellsworth before Torgerson did.

It was one more worry in an already worrisome day.

Chapter 11

Abel Kane was surprised that his brother Jock had taken the trail boss job for Becker. When Torgerson told him, Abel had concealed his surprise and played dumb. But now it was something he had to think about.

How was he supposed to know that damned Twyla had a bad ticker? Nobody told him about her heart. All he'd wanted was a little taste of that sugar. Besides, he was drunk and Jock hadn't ought to have blamed him for something that came natural to a man. Twyla was one good-looking woman and she made a lot of heads turn. Men's and women's.

He had seen the murderous look in Jock's eyes when Twyla had died. It made him shudder now to think of it. But he hadn't meant any harm to Twyla. Jock just didn't understand. It was living out there on that ranch, so far from town, working so hard every day from can't see to can't see, and then having that beautiful woman around. Jock's woman.

Abel hadn't meant to do anything more to Twyla than to kiss her. But when she resisted, that made him all the more excited—then it became a challenge. He had wanted more, and he was half drunk and sexed up, so he just went ahead and put the boots to her. Then Jock had come in and caught them. It was a blur after that—he remembered hearing Twyla say something, then she was crying and Jock was holding her in his arms, shouting at him. He had heard Jock say he was going to kill him for what he did, so Abel lit a shuck. He knew his brother that much. If Jock said something, he sure as hell meant it.

But now it seemed he couldn't get far enough away from Jock, no matter how hard he tried. Maybe Jock wasn't hunting him, exactly, but sooner or later Jock would find out where he was. That was what he rode with now—the knowledge that Jock would track him down and exact revenge for Twyla's death.

Abel cursed aloud, just thinking of those

things. Thinking of Twyla and how she had fought him and how he had taken her anyway, knowing he had no right, but knowing she had been taunting him with her beauty and driving him crazy with the way she walked and talked and moved. Damn her. Damn Jock.

He was used to the darkness. It gave him comfort now. In the distance, a choir of coyotes wafted their song across the plain, and it sent a thrill through him for some unknown reason. There was enough light from the stars and the rising moon so that Abel easily found his way back to where he had been riding the flank with Randy Clutter. Randy was there when Abel rode up, and the herd was moving along steadily, grazing just enough to keep the cows satisfied. As long as they had something to chew on, the cows seemed content.

"What was that all about?" Randy asked when Abel rode up. "Torgerson wanted to see you, right. About what?"

"Randy, you ask too damned many questions at once," Abel said. "I can't handle more'n one at a time."

"Well, what's going on? What did Torgerson want with you?"

The coyote chorus stopped abruptly, as if a door had been slammed shut on a room.

None of the notes lingered. The night took on an eerie cast, as if something of its essence had been taken away, leaving only a shadow of what once was. Abel listened, not trusting his ears, but the silence was absolute beyond the sound of the cattle in the foreground. In the distance, there was only a deep silence, that subtraction of music that had floated on the night air.

"My bud's hooked up with Becker," Abel said.

"Huh?"

"You heard me. Jock's riding for the X8 brand."

"I thought your brother was still back in Del Rio."

"You ain't the brightest lamp on the street, are you, Randy? I said Jock was hired on as trail boss for Becker. You got that?"

"Yeah, but how come Torgerson sent for you? Did he fire you?"

"Hell, no, he didn't fire me. Shit, you ask a lot of questions, Randy. You ought to have been born a woman."

"That ain't funny, Abel. I'm just curious is all."

"Well, be curious about something else. I don't want to talk about what Torgerson said or did. Hear?"

"Well, all right. I mean, if it's a damned old secret."

Abel touched spurs to his horse's flanks, dancing it a few feet ahead of Clutter.

"It ain't no secret. He just asked me if I knew that Jock had joined up with the X8 is all."

"How come? I mean why would Torgerson want to know that?"

Abel slowed his horse. He snorted in disgust, and speared Randy with a look that he knew the other man could not see. He felt his anger burning in him, burning, just about to burst into a raging flame.

"Do you know what the hell loyalty is, Randy?"

Clutter hesitated. Swallowed. Even in the dim light, Abel could see his Adam's apple bob in his throat.

"I never thought about it much, I reckon," Randy said.

"Well, maybe you ought to. Didn't you never feel you owed somebody something? Maybe someone did you a good turn and you felt obligated to that person?"

"No, I reckon not. What's that got to do with that other thing? That royalty."

"Not royalty, Randy. Loyalty. Do you know what being loyal is?"

"Maybe."

"Maybe, my ass. You don't have the least idea of what the word means."

"I got a pretty good idea. I just never used it much. Never heard it much, neither. Not until tonight, when you said it."

"Well, Randy, though I ain't a teacher, and sure ain't your teacher, I'm going to tell you what loyalty is, you dumbbell."

"You don't need to be calling me no names, neither, Abel Kane."

"When you ride for the brand, that means you don't never walk away from it while you're drawing pay from the outfit. Loyalty means you stick with the brand no matter what."

"So, what's that got to do with your brother and Mr. Torgerson?"

Abel shook his head. "I swear, Randy, sometimes you're like a burr under a blanket."

"There you go again. Calling me names, Abel."

"No, I ain't calling you no names. Listen, Randy, Torgerson just wanted to know where I stood with my brother, that's all. He wondered if I'd be loyal to him or to Jock."

"Well, you and Jock had a falling out, didn't you? That was a dumb question."

"Not really. Torgerson doesn't know about my fight with Jock. He just wanted to know, if push came to shove on this here drive, if I would side with Jock or with him."

"And what did you tell him?"

"Shit, Randy. You just keep on, don't you?"

"Hell, I said I was curious."

"Well, what in hell do you think I said to Torgerson? Huh? Do you think I told him that if my brother rode up here and told me to steal all the Cross J cattle and give them to him, I'd just do it?"

"Naw, I didn't think that, Abel. I just thought . . ."

Randy didn't complete the sentence and Abel thought he might have gotten off the hook with Randy's questions. He wanted to let it drop right there, but he knew he had not made his point. With Randy, you always had to nail down what was left flapping in the breeze.

"Randy, Torgerson just thought what everybody thinks. That blood is thicker than water. He might have wondered about me riding over to the X8 herd because my brother was ramrodding it. And, if I did, he wanted it to be sooner, rather than later."

"Well, golly, Abel, you might."

"Might what?"

"Want to work with your brother, like you used to back in Del Rio. Before you and me and D.F. went into robbing folks. Before Jock almost caught us that one time."

Abel stiffened. "You shut up about that, Randy."

"Huh?"

"What we did back in Del Rio ain't nobody's business and you, me and D.F. don't talk about those things no more. Hear?"

"Yeah. Well, nobody knows. I mean, your brother never found out. He almost did."

"Just shut the hell up."

"You don't need to get on me like that, Abel. Hell, you don't know the half of it, anyways."

"What do you mean?" Abel bristled. That was another thing he had tried to forget. And now Randy had brought it up again, out of nowhere. After Jock had lost his herd up in Kansas, Abel and he had fallen on hard times. No money. No fun. Jock took it a lot better, but Abel had fallen in with Randy and Dan Fogarty. They had taken to robbery to finance their nights at the saloon. One neighbor had asked Jock to help him track some stolen horses, not knowing that the three of them had stolen the animals and were going to sell them over in Mexico for some beer money. But Jock had tracked them and almost caught them. Abel had told D.F. and Randy that they had to let the horses go and light a shuck out of there, or else Jock would catch them. D.F. agreed, but Randy had gotten mad that they were going to lose out, after all that hard work.

"I near dropped the hammer on your brother that time we were running those horses over the border."

"What?"

"Yeah. But I wondered if you'd get mad if I dropped old Jock so's we could keep those horses, get us some cash money."

"So, that's where you were. Dan and I thought you had got caught. Worried us sick until you showed up."

"I had old Jock plumb in my sights, Abel. Yeah, I could have dropped him so easy. But you wouldn't have done nothing, right? Hell, we could have sold them horses to that army guy in Mexico."

That was before Abel had taken after Twyla. Now he wondered just what he would have done if Randy had killed Jock. He had wanted Twyla a lot even then, but he hadn't gone after her. Not then.

"Randy, if you had killed Jock that day, you wouldn't be sitting on that horse jawing with me."

"Huh?"

"You heard me. I would have shot you dead if you had put a bullet in Jock."

"Well, D.F. wanted to do it, too. Maybe you did yourself. I don't know."

"No, not then I didn't."

"What about now, Abel? What if Jock was to ride up right now and I shot him out of the saddle—would you shoot me?"

"Randy, sometimes you get on a man's nerves. But that's the same question Torgerson asked me. Pretty much the same question."

"What? He asked you if you'd kill your own brother?"

"Yeah."

"Well, there you are, Abel. Things sure change, huh? What did you tell Torgerson?"

"None of your business, Randy."

"Bullshit. You told him you'd kill your own brother, didn't you?"

"Shut up, Randy. For the last damned time. Just shut up."

Randy kept quiet. But Abel knew he was studying on that last question of his and maybe someday Abel would have to answer him.

Maybe, someday, he'd find out if he really *could* kill his own brother.

Chapter 12

Jock held his breath a lot for the first three days of the drive. The herd moved slowly over the plain, drifting like a great river; expanding, contracting, flowing over a course Jock had selected, grazing as it walked to the north, fifteen thousand head of multicolored longhorns.

The young drovers worked well, Jock thought, letting the cattle find their way to the best grass, but keeping them all in a bunch despite the length and breadth of their numbers. He was pleased that there had been no stampedes, no mass exodus of cattle turning back to the home range. He thought that this might have been because he did not hurry the lead cow and made sure there was plenty of water along the route, and good bedding grounds at night.

Jock wondered, however, how long his luck could hold with such a huge herd.

They had made only five or six miles a day and Jock sensed that Chad was fretting at the slowness. But he couldn't be too mindful about that. Chad had his schedule in mind, but the herd also had a schedule, and so did Jock. Very seldom, he knew, would they all mesh.

Chad rode alongside him now as they ranged far ahead of the slow-moving herd. The ever-present cigarette dangled from Jock's parched lips, the smoke scouring his eyes with almost sentient tendrils, burning them until they protected themselves with tears.

"At this rate," Chad said, "we'll make Ellsworth next spring."

So, he was fretting, Jock thought.

"Be a nice time of year in Kansas."

"It's not funny, Jocko. We've got to make more miles a day or we'll lose out on the sale."

Jock was looking ahead and not paying full attention to what Chad was saying. At times he wished Chad had stayed at home with his wife and daughter. He wasn't exactly a nuisance yet, but he was getting there, getting under Jock's skin like a chigger itch.

"We'll get there, Chad. In due time."

"Not at this speed, we won't."

"Just think of how fat your cattle are getting," Jock said. "That's one thing about longhorns. They can graze on bare land and fatten up like sows."

Becker had good stock, Jock knew. Besides the mix of the Spanish *retinto* with American stock, there were mixes of the Mexican *criollo*, and even some red-and-white-peppered *sabinas*, mixed in with the brindles, blue roans, mulberries, Jersey creams, mouse-colored, lots of duns in various shades, speckled blues, ring-streaked, wild-eyed, rangy steers and cows, a bunch of red roans, some bays with brown points, browns with bay points, even some solid blacks, along with blacks that were splotched with red, brown or white. There were even some white longhorns, ghostly and lean, tall and big-horned, and many pale reds that looked as if their colors had faded in the wash. Chad had almost the entire history of longhorn cattle grown on both sides of the border, and maybe some breeds mixed in from Kentucky or Virginia so long ago that nobody knew where they had come from, or how.

"I just need to get them up to Ellsworth before Torgerson runs his herd into the stockyards," Chad said, a bitter edge to his voice.

"Well, from the looks of that ground up ahead, Torgerson has already passed this way, a few days ago, and left nothing but sprigs for this herd to feed on."

"What?" Chad stood up in his stirrups and stared ahead in the direction Jock was pointing. The ground was churned up from the passage of many cloven hooves and there was so little green to be seen that he had to strain to see any of it.

"We'll have to go west or east from here," Jock said.

"That bastard."

Jock laughed and ashes collapsed from the end of his cigarette, vanishing into the silk of the slight breeze wafting over the plain.

Chad looked at the ground more closely as they reached the point where Torgerson had apparently started on the trail north. The ground showed the stamp of many hooves and the stench of manure was strong in his nostrils. The grass looked as if a horde of locusts had descended upon it. Pulled-up roots lay here and there, their tendrils tangled with daubs of dirt that had already dried and would soon turn to dust.

"More water to the west," Jock said. "More grass, too. And maybe we can get ahead of Torgerson. Flank him."

"You make it sound like a race, Jock."

"Well, ain't it?" Jock cracked, a smile flickering on his lips.

Chad let out a sigh as Jock turned his horse and set out toward the west. He turned and waved to the man riding point on the herd, Fred Naylor. Naylor put the spurs to his horse and rode toward Becker.

"We'll turn the herd here, Fred," Chad said. "Head for the sunset."

"I can see why," Naylor said, glancing at the ground all around them.

"See you at supper," Chad said, and took off after Jock. A few minutes before he caught up, Chad doubled over in the saddle, struck by a sudden spasm of pain. He pulled out the small bottle in his pocket and drank a swallow. Sweat beaded up on his forehead. His eyes squinted as he fought down the pain that felt like a knife being twisted in his stomach. He swore under his breath until the agony subsided, then put the bottle back in his pocket and wiped his face with the bandanna he wore around his neck. His eyes glazed over as a last twinge of pain shot through his innards like a hot lance.

Jock turned around when Chad rode up beside him, and saw his friend's ashen face.

"What's the matter, Chad? You don't look so good."

"I'm all right," Chad said tightly. "Just a cramp."

"Maybe you ought to take it easy. I can scout on my own."

Chad waved a hand in objection. "No, no, I'm all right. The bad part's already passed."

"The bad part? What have you got, anyway? You look pretty peaked. Like somebody put a fist in your gut."

Chad shook his head and tried to smile. The spasms had passed, but he felt weak.

"Ain't you ever had a bellyache, Jock?"

"Oh, yeah. That what you got?"

"A little one. Something I ate, likely."

Jock could see that Chad didn't want to talk about it, but he knew there was more to Chad's condition than a simple bellyache. He had seen him go off by himself after supper and come back to the camp with that same haggard look, that same pained expression on his face. Chad was hiding something, not only from him, but from himself. He put it in the back of his mind and vowed to pay closer attention to Chad's spells.

They rode on in silence for a time, following a line of hoof marks in the ground that showed where Torgerson's herd had passed two or three days earlier. Five or six miles later, Jock saw the line end and rode onto untouched ground where the grass was more plentiful. The route would take them ten or twelve miles out of their way, but it could have been worse.

What he saw next was more ominous, though, and he almost missed it.

Jock didn't say anything at first. He wanted to be sure. But a sidelong glance at the ground revealed a lone hoofprint of an un-shod pony. Chad was looking up at the sky, and ahead toward the endless prairie stretching to the north. He hadn't seen it, and he didn't seem to notice when Jock turned his horse to ride in the direction of the horse track.

Jock wondered if the pony had been following some predetermined route or whether the rider was a scout just roaming that part of the country. The track gradually turned from the north to the east and Jock followed it, noting that it was fresher than the cow tracks left by Torgerson's herd.

"Where you going, Jock?" Chad asked. "Seems to me like we're doubling back."

"Following pony tracks."

"Pony tracks?"

"Seems like we got company, maybe. Or Torgerson has. Only one set of tracks so far, but if he's a scout, he's looking for beefsteak on the hoof."

Jock pointed to the tracks. They were plain to see, even from atop a horse.

Chad's eyes widened and he swallowed a gob of saliva that had welled up in his mouth. "One Indian," he said. "Doesn't mean much."

"I'll follow them on out, Chad. They look to be a couple of days old."

"That's not getting my herd where it ought to be."

Jock shrugged. "You're the boss, Chad. When I see pony tracks, I think of trouble."

"They're old, you say, and they're not anywhere near my herd. Let's go on. Let Torgerson worry about it."

"Suit yourself," Jock said, and turned his horse.

He rode back to where he had picked up the pony tracks and continued westward, then turned north. They came to a creek and Jock rode along its banks one way and then the other.

"We'll bed the herd down here tonight," Jock said. "That all right?"

"Looks good. Plenty of grass and water. I'll ride back and mark the trail."

"Good. I'll see you this evening, Chad. Ride careful."

"I will," Chad said.

Jock watched him go and breathed a single sigh of relief. He knew he should have followed those tracks out, but it didn't matter. When he had ridden up the creek, he had seen many more signs of unshod ponies. He hadn't said anything to Chad. No need to worry him at this point.

But he would set extra watches that night because he had found the place where the Indians—Apaches, most likely—had crossed the creek. And that was only after the bunch of them had been joined by the man who made those lone tracks behind Torgerson's herd.

The Apaches had crossed the creek and were waiting somewhere to the north. He was sure of that because the others had not ridden east after the Torgerson herd. For some reason, they would be waiting for the cattle of the X8, probably because they were moving so slowly.

It was just a hunch, but Jock crossed over the creek and saw where the tracks led. They did not lead in the direction of Torgerson's herd, but went due northwest.

And that was just where he was going with this herd.

Jock rolled a cigarette and lit it. Then he looked up at the sun and marked its place in the sky. His nerves were twanging like a guitar with a broken string.

Chapter 13

While waiting by the creek for the herd to come in, Jock began working out some tactics that he hoped would overcome any Apache trouble they might encounter. He thought he could find the right kind of men to perform the tasks he would assign; men he had been watching and assessing for the past few days. He was sure he could find those he needed.

That night at bed-down, Jock began talking to some of the men as they came to the chuck wagon for chow.

"I'm going to need a few men to act as scouts," he said to each group in turn. "I need good trackers and good shots."

Jock asked each group who they thought was the best tracker in the outfit. The name that kept coming up was a man they called Horky.

Horky, he learned, was Julio Horcasitas, a young, keen-eyed Mexican who had a reputation as a hunter and tracker of game.

"Horky," Jock said when the man came into camp for supper, "I hear you can read sign."

"Sign?"

"Tracks. Animal tracks."

"Yes, my father taught me."

"What about Indians? Ever track any Indians?"

"I have seen their moccasin tracks many times. I have seen the tracks of their ponies. I saw some today. Many tracks."

Jock smiled. "Are you a good shot?"

"He's a good shot," one of the men said.

Jock turned and saw Amos Beeson, one of the drovers, sitting down with a plate full of beans and beef, leaning against one of the wagon wheels.

"That right?" Jock said.

"Horky can pick a blackbird off a cattail at a hunnert yards," Beeson said. "I seen him do it once't."

Horky's lips wrinkled in a shy grin.

"That right, Horky?" Jock asked.

"I think maybe so. If Amos say so."

"I do," Beeson said.

"How would you feel about leading some men as outriders to hunt for Apache sign?" Jock asked. He watched Horky closely for any sign of hesitation or fear.

"If Mr. Becker say so, I will do this."

"I'm the boss on the trail here, Horky."

"If you want me to do this, I will do it."

"Good. Amos, you can ride with Horky, and I'll get a couple more men to go with you."

"What do you want us to do if we run into Apaches, Kane? Get into a fight with them?" Beeson laced his words with sarcasm, but Jock thought that he probably would have reacted the same way.

"If you find fresh tracks, or you actually see any Apaches," Jock said, "just let me know. I don't want you to risk your lives."

"Well, if I see an Apache," Beeson said, "I'm going to throw down on the bastard. I run into them before, when I was a boy, and they're pure meanness, I tell you true."

"You can settle that among yourselves," Jock said. "If you're jumped, attacked, you'll have to defend yourselves. All right, Horky?"

"All right," Horky said.

Jock wondered if Horky had ever killed a man, but he wasn't going to ask. The young man seemed willing enough.

"I'll send you out tomorrow," Jock said. "You won't have to drive cattle until we find out what the Apaches have in mind. I saw their tracks, too," he said to Horky.

Before the night was over Jock had selected three teams of three men each to man his patrols. With Horky and Beeson, he put Earl Foster. Another team had Ed Purvis, Pablo Cornejo and Fred Naylor. The final group he sent out consisted of Lou Quist, Gilberto Fuentes and Dub Morley. He told them that he would expect them to check back in every two hours, and report to him what they had seen or not seen.

"If you get in trouble and can't send a man back to me, fire a rifle off three times, fast as you can," he told them. "We'll bring help."

He checked the men's weapons the next morning. Each had a sidearm, and each had a rifle. Some had Sharps carbines. One or two had heavy Henry repeating rifles, but there was a rolling block and an Enfield among them.

"Are you sure this is wise?" Chad asked, when the three patrols left at sunup.

"Just a precaution, Chad."

"Puts us right short of drovers."

"We can manage," Jock said.

"How come you sent Quist out? Lou won't

do you no favors. And why put him with Dub Morley? Dub's got about as much work in him as a strawless broom."

"Quist is carrying a big grudge," Jock said. "Maybe some of it will wear off if he beats some brush. And he's not afraid of anything or anyone. I figure if he gets into a fight, he'll give a good account of himself. As for Dub, I got personal reasons for sending him out."

"Mind telling me what those reasons are, Jock?"

"I've been watching him work cattle, Chad. I can't prove it, but I think he's been responsible for some of the tangles we've had on the drive. Every time the herd kinks up and starts to stray, I hear explanations from the other drovers that Dub is the one who pulled the cork out of the bottle. Either he's just a poor drover with poor judgment, or he's deliberately trying to slow this herd down."

"You could be right. I don't know Dub all that well."

"Do you know if he ever worked for Torgerson?" Jock asked.

Chad shook his head. "All I know is we signed him on late."

"Well, could be Torgerson sent him over to you just to be a thorn in your side."

"I don't know, Jock. I just don't know."

"Dub's better off away from this herd. I just don't want him anywhere near your cows for a while."

"You're the boss."

The herd was moving and Jock ranged well ahead, alone, leaving Chad to manage the drovers, seeing that the herd stayed together. Some of the men were grumbling already, but he knew the cattle were settled down and moving well. The men would do the same. Idle hands were the devil's workshop, he thought with a wry smile. Give the men something to do and they would forget they were short several hands. But he knew this would be a day when the hands would be long on sweat and short on tempers.

Jock rolled a cigarette once he was well away from the leading edge of the herd, lit it and turned his head so that smoke didn't sting his eyes. But he was looking at the ground, too, checking the horse tracks of the men he had sent out. He kept tracks in his mind and he had made sure to mark those of every scout he had chosen. He had always kept tracks in his mind; at least, ever since his father had first taught him how to track deer, javelina, quail and turkey. Tracks fascinated him as a child and he used to draw them in books to remember them. But there came a time when he no longer needed to draw them. He could remember tracks, each with its own distinctions, its own peculiarities.

"If you can track," his father once told him, "you'll never get lost and you'll never starve. Tracks are messages the game leaves for the hunter to read."

And his tracking ability had stood him in good stead when he was with the Second Texas. He was often sent out to scout enemy positions and look for signs of patrols. He took pride in his tracking ability and had been surprised when he discovered how easy it was to track men and their horses. He could tell when soldiers stopped to rest or take a piss or do grunt, and their cigarettes always told a story: whether or not they were in a hurry, or how careless they were. Or nervous. When he saw cigarettes half smoked, he knew the rider was either startled by something or jumpy, especially when he found more than one tossed away before the smoker had finished.

His father had taught him to track ants and doodlebugs, making him lie down on his belly and study a small piece of ground until he was able to tell the story of every small creature that was there or had been there. He learned to study the grasses and the dirt from close up and then from atop a horse, or just walking along. At first he had not seen the sense in it, but after a time, he saw the wisdom in the exercises his father gave him. The earth was alive and most people didn't notice the small things, and the small things were often the most telling, the most important. He learned how to tell the age of a track by studying how much dirt had drifted in since it had been made or how much dew or rain was in it. A blade of grass would always try to bend back toward the sun, and he could tell how long ago such a blade had been stepped on by an animal or a man, and how heavy either one was.

All of the horse tracks faded away as the scouts rode off in different directions. He hoped they would know where he'd be when it came time for them to report. He had given them specific instructions about that part of their duties, explaining to them how to figure dead reckoning and how to calculate his speed and direction. A lot of it was by guess and by gosh, he knew, but the good scouts should be able to find him pretty easily.

Quail piped in the distance and Jock listened carefully. An Apache could imitate a bobwhite perfectly, he knew, and they knew the difference between the calls of male and female. It was sometimes difficult to tell the real thing from an imitation.

It was quiet for a time and his cigarette burned down until the tobacco was too hot to draw on, so he spit out the ragged and soggy butt. He was considering whether or not to roll another one when he heard another quail off to his left. Then came an answering call from another direction.

Jock stiffened in the saddle and loosened his Sharps carbine in its scabbard.

Neither call had been made by a bobwhite.

He looked up at the sun, marking the approximate time of day. He had been riding for about two hours and none of the scouts had shown up to report. That wasn't crucial at this point, he knew.

But the quail calls had not been made by any quail, either.

Jock looked all around, standing up in the stirrups to stretch his length of view. He saw nothing but prairie, but the calls had made his scalp prickle. He slowed his horse, then reined it to a stop.

He listened.

Then, another quail call. Very close this time.

He started to ride toward it as he pulled his rifle from its sheath. Then he heard the crack of a rifle not far away. One shot, followed by two others from the same gun—by the sound of it a Henry repeating rifle.

The shots were followed by the high-pitched screeches of Indians, just over a rise.

Jock recognized those sounds. They were the war cries of Apache braves and he knew they weren't hunting buffalo.

Chapter 14

Jock rode toward the crackle of rifle fire. The high-pitched yelps of the Apaches punctuated the crack of rifles. As he topped the rise, he saw puffs of white smoke shredding like gauze in the breeze. At first he could see no horses or riders, but then he saw an orange flash and heard the sizzle of a bullet as it fried the air next to his right ear.

The shot came from the right, but the Apaches were on his left. He saw them a split second later, rising up from the ground, shooting, then scurrying off to reload or hide. He smelled the acrid scent of burnt powder as he rode into the smoke, hunched over his saddle so that he made a smaller target.

He fired at one Apache and missed. Still, the Indians did not turn their guns on him, but continued to direct their fire at the shoot-ers to the east. Jock rode that way, making a wide circle so that he could come up behind the X8 hands. He thought that one of them might have mistaken him for an Apache when he rode up, and he didn't want that to happen again.

"It's me, Jock Kane," he called when he came up on a half dozen men lying prone on the ground behind a low rise. Their horses were tied to mesquite bushes a hundred yards or so behind them. As he got there, one of them turned and looked at him. It was Lou Quist.

"Put your horse up, Kane, and help us out," Quist said.

"Be right there."

Jock rode back and tied his horse with the others. He dug into his saddlebags for more cartridges for the Sharps, then, hunching over, he made his way back to the fighting.

Horky's bunch was there, with Quist's, but Jock noticed that one man wasn't moving. He looked more closely and saw blood covering one side of the man's face in a smear. He winced, not recognizing who it was, but knowing that the man was dead. He counted heads and that was even more puzzling. All six of the scouts from Horky and Quist's bunches were there, sprawled on the ground like army snipers. He crawled up beside Horky, and laid his rifle out in front of him, resting it on a clod of dirt.

"How many, Horky?"

"I do not know for sure, boss. Maybe seven or eight, I think."

"Who got killed?"

"I do not know. I think he was with the Apaches. Dub, he shot him. It all happened so fast."

"They jump you?"

"Yes. They came out of the ground, I think. We dragged the body here, trying to make him breathe. But, he died."

"I smell something," Jock said. "Beef?"

"They were cooking a steer when we rode up. I fired my rifle three times and Quist came to help us."

Bullets whizzed overhead, and once in a while one of the drovers fired at a target. The Apaches were moving around, but they weren't leaving. They smelled blood and maybe they wanted scalps. Jock knew that they couldn't stay there, pinned down as they were. Sooner or later, the Apaches would flank them or rush them and it would be a bloody mess.

"We can't fight them lying here on our bellies," Jock said. "We need to get back on our horses."

"Every time we try to do that, they shoot much," Horky said.

Jock sniffed the air. Besides the smell of cooked beef, there were the aromas of burning wood and cowpies. He tried to put together a picture of what had happened. The Apaches had stolen a beef and were cooking the best parts when the scouts came up on them. The Indians must have been very hungry. But, from where had they stolen a cow to cook, way out here on the plain? From the X8 herd? Not likely. But he knew he had better find out. He hadn't expected his men to find a bunch of Apaches cooking meat in the middle of nowhere. Rather, he had thought they might run into a scouting party and then put them on the run. Instead, they were in a fight and the Apaches had drawn first blood.

"Hell, we can't see 'em," Morley said. "That last bullet was too damned close."

"Dub, shut up," Quist said, and shot his rifle at a flash of color some sixty yards away.

"Where in hell did the Apaches get all that ammunition?" Jock said aloud, asking no one but himself. As if in reply, the Apaches sent a volley of shots their way. The bullets plowed furrows in the ground just in front of the lined-up men, and sand stung the faces of some of them.

"We've got to get the hell out of here," Jock said, loud enough for all the men to hear. "Crawl backward to your horses. I'll hold the Apaches off from here."

"They might rush you and kill you, boss," Horky said.

"Want me to stay with you, boss?" Beeson asked.

Jock shook his head. "No, get moving. Just scoot backward until you think you can make a run for your horses. I'll keep fire on the Apaches."

"Here," Beeson said. "Maybe this Henry will do you more good. It has sixteen or seventeen cartridges in it. That ought to be enough."

Beeson handed Jock the Henry. It was a big, heavy Yellow Boy. Jock handed over his carbine to Beeson.

"Good luck, Jocko," Beeson said, and Jock welcomed the familiarity. It was a tight situation and he hoped he had the courage to face up to the challenge. The odds were not in his favor, he knew.

He worked the lever on the Henry, and saw that there was a cartridge already loaded in the chamber. He closed the breech, and waited. He heard the men scooting backward, the noise of their denims rubbing against dirt, rock, and brush.

Jock held the rifle steady, looking for movement. He saw the smoke from the Apache cookfire, just a thin, wispy tendril rising in the air. So, he knew where the Apaches had been when the scouts had encountered them. Now he looked for movement on either side of the pigtail of smoke, and when he saw a head pop up, he squeezed the trigger and sent a round burning over the Apache's head. He levered another cartridge into the chamber, heard the metallic clunk as the empty hull ejected and spanged against a pebble before coming to rest in the dirt.

The head bobbed back down and disappeared.

As he listened, Jock heard soft voices speaking in another language, which he took to be Apache. It wasn't Spanish, he knew that. Then he heard the scuffle of unshod hooves and knew that one or more of the Indians was either moving the ponies or preparing to mount up.

Memories of the war came rushing in on Jock. Other battles, sieges. Not like this one, but every bit as nerve-wracking. Hearing the enemy, but not seeing the enemy. His palms began to sweat and the smell of the dirt beneath his body conjured up old fears; fears of dying on a battlefield all alone, blown to bits by a mortar or cannon round and nothing but pieces left scattered in all directions.

He could almost smell the blood of the dead man nearby, and maybe he could smell him, because his senses were so acute, so tightly honed as he faced, once again, his own mortality. Life hung by so fragile a thread in battle. Every breath became precious, every thought could be the last, and yet they were so jumbled up, they didn't matter. Maybe it was only the smell of death that kept a man alive, gave him the courage to face the same death that lay next to him, or a few yards away, with vacant eyes and drying blood and the stench of voided bowels that came with sudden death, when a man's sphincter muscle relaxed and let his grunt out for all to smell, for all to take heed of as a warning of what might lie ahead in the blinding, clinging white smoke, in the terrible rattle of grapeshot or the angry whine of a minié ball slicing through the air, looking for a man's body to splay and smash to that final oblivion.

The yipping had stopped and Jock knew, with a sudden shock, that he had not heard the Apache yells for some time. When had it stopped? Before he rode up, he knew. Usually those high-pitched screeches meant that the Indians were on the attack. So, when had the attack stopped? And why?

His skin began to crawl with the realization that he was all alone, facing an unseen enemy. Behind him were the men he had chosen as scouts. If the Apaches were to rush him and he had to run, he could be caught in the crossfire, perhaps even killed by one of his own hands.

Jock strained to hear, but there was only a deep silence. He no longer heard the shuffling of hooves from the Apache ponies. Were the Indians sneaking off? Had they already left? He could see no sign of movement from where he lay. His scalp prickled as if a spider egg had hatched on the back of his neck.

He didn't dare turn around to see where his men were now. Had they reached the horses? No, probably not, or he would hear them riding up. The minutes crawled by in agonizing slowness.

Jock knew he could no longer stay where he was. The Apaches could be anywhere. They could be circling to come up on his men from behind, or they could be flanking him, and them, on both sides. He knew he had to get back to his own horse. From where he lay, he was a sitting duck, with no defenses beyond a borrowed Henry rifle and the Colt he wore on his hip.

He scooted backward, keeping the rifle up out of the dirt and pointed in the general direction of where he had last seen movement on the Apache side. Back, back, back, he crawled, expecting an attack at any moment.

His progress was slow. Very slow. He didn't even know if he was moving in a straight line. He didn't dare look back to see where he was going, where the other men were. He tried to keep his alignment on course the way he saw it.

The silence was immense and deep.

Then he heard it and his blood turned to ice.

A high-pitched Apache yell broke the silence, and then it was joined by a chorus of screeches that sounded like an overwhelming horde of Apaches heading straight for him in a do-or-die charge.

In front of him, an Apache rose from the ground, his face smeared with dirt and paint, his mouth open in a blood-curdling scream. He had a pistol in his hand and it was spurting lead and flame from the barrel. He ran toward Jock like a deer, bounding high and zigzagging with astonishing agility.

137

Jock took aim, knowing that in a few seconds the Apache would be right on top of him, firing at point-blank range. It seemed that his heart stopped in that long moment. His finger curled around the trigger of the Henry and he tried to draw a bead on the charging Apache. He held his breath for what seemed an eternity. Then Jock squeezed the trigger, hoping he had figured right, hoping the Apache would run straight into the bullet fired from the Henry. The explosion in his ears drowned out all other sound and the butt of the rifle bucked hard against his shoulder.

The Apache did not break stride as he aimed the pistol in his hand straight at Jock's head and squeezed the trigger.

Chapter 15

The onrushing Apache's last cry was torn from his throat as Jock's bullet smashed into his chest, the lead flattening against bone and flesh, ripping through arteries and heart like some metal fist. The Apache's pistol shot went wild, thudding into dirt, cracking rock and burying itself in the ground. The Apache pitched forward, blood spurting from the small hole in his chest, gushing from a peach-pit-sized hole in his back where it tore out ribs and meat, churning them to fragments of pulp.

Jock levered another cartridge into the rifle's chamber and got to his feet, expecting more Apaches to rush him. Instead, he saw a gaggle of ponies racing off to the south, Apache riders silent as ghosts in full flight.

He counted six braves atop the ponies, all of them brandishing rifles.

A moment later he heard hoofbeats from behind him and turned to see his scouts riding toward him. Horky was leading Jock's horse. From where they were, Jock knew they could not see the retreating Apaches yet, and by the time they reached him, the Indians would be out of sight.

Jock walked over to the Apache he had shot. He touched the toe of his boot to the man's side. He lay still, stone dead, the bleeding halted with the failed pumping of his heart. Jock felt sadness wash over him, like the sadness at Corinth when he had killed a Union soldier at close range. He did not like taking a man's life, robbing a living person of his future on earth. It made him feel as if a part of him had been lost.

He turned and looked at the other dead man, wondering who he was and why he had been there, so close to the Apaches, if not actually one of their number.

Horky rode up and handed Jock the reins to his horse.

"Looks like you chased them off," Beeson said.

"I didn't chase them off, Amos. This one came after me and I shot him. I think he sacrificed his life so that the others could escape. Otherwise, it makes no sense."

"It makes sense, all right," Quist said. "Them murderin' bastards knew they was outnumbered. If we'd have got here in time, we'd have turned all of them cowardly savages into wolf meat."

"I don't think they ran because of cowardice," Jock said. "I think they had other things on their minds."

"Oh, yeah?" Quist said. "Like what?"

"I don't know. But I want to take a look at that beef they butchered."

Dub's face paled, and Jock noticed it.

Jock mounted his horse and rode to where the Apaches had been camped. The others followed in somber procession, the smell of death thick in the air.

A small fire was still smoldering, and the scent of roasted meat lingered. A large longhorn cow lay nearby, disemboweled, but the hide still on it. Jock swung down, and handed his reins to Horky.

"I'm going to take a look," Jock said. "Just sit tight, all of you. Those Apaches might come back." Jock handed up the Henry to Beeson and retrieved his own Sharps repeater. "Thanks, Beeson. It shoots right true."

Everyone went on the alert. There was a

rattling of rifles and the snap of lever actions as the scouts scanned the surrounding landscape.

The Indians had cut off the head of the cow and placed it on a small mound, facing east. It sat there like some hideous artifact, its eyes bristling with flies, its tongue cut out, its neck flecked with dried blotches of blood. Its tongueless mouth gaped as if the animal had been frozen in the midst of a silent scream. Its horns were dug into the ground to balance the head, and dirt had been scooped up behind its neck to hold the entire body part in a semirigid position.

Jock kicked the head off its perch, grabbed one horn and rolled it over until the skull was facedown. Flies boiled up in a swarm as Jock turned his back on the desecrated shrine.

He walked over to the carcass and knelt down to examine it. The cow had been gutted expertly, the liver and heart removed, its stomach and entrails lying beside it in a grotesque puddle. The stench of the intestines rose up and assaulted Jock's nostrils.

The Apaches had begun cutting into the cow's haunch. The tendons and muscles were partially severed. Jock passed his hand over the hide on the cow's hip and then leaned over, checking the brand. He looked at it hard, then looked again. He stood and walked back to his horse. He took the reins from Horky and mounted up.

"Any of you see that brand?" Jock asked.

The men all shook their heads.

"Well, it's not an X8."

"It ain't?" Beeson said. "What is it?"

"It's a Cross J brand."

Jock rode over to the dead white man with the others following. He looked down at the man's face, what was left of it. He had been shot in the head and so the features were distorted. But there was a clean, black hole where the bullet had entered, and streaks of blood that were now dried almost black.

"Anybody know this jasper?" Jock asked.

He reined his horse away from the dead man so that the others could file by and look at him. Dub Morley hung back and was the last to pass next to the corpse. But he hardly gave it a glance, Jock noticed.

"That looks like Pip Boggs," Quist said. "Can't be sure, though."

"P. P. Boggs. Yeah, I thought that's who he looks like," Beeson said. "Didn't you and him used to work together on the old Rocking R, Dub?"

"It don't look like Pip," Morley said.

"Look again, Dub," Jock said.

Morley turned his horse around and forced himself to look at the dead man.

"I don't know," Dub said.

"Well, you shot him, didn't you?" Jock said.

There was a stretch of silence. All the other scouts looked at Dub Morley. Their looks were accusatory, hard and searching.

"I thought he was with them Apaches," Morley said lamely.

Jock looked at the other men. His eyes glittered like crushed diamonds in the sunlight. "Did any of you think this man was with the Apaches?"

Some of the men nodded quickly. Others, more reluctantly. Morley was the first to nod, perhaps because Jock still had him fixed with his stare like a butterfly to a piece of cardboard.

"I see that Boggs's pistol is still in his holster," Jock said. "He didn't have his rifle out, either."

His words drew only silence from the men. Jock knew he wasn't going to get anywhere with these men, who were still rattled from the encounter with the Apaches.

"Quist, you and Horky track down those Apaches. See where they're going. Be careful.

I think this bunch was just part of a bigger one."

"If they are," Quist said, "we can't do much."

"No," Jock admitted, "you can't. Nor do I want you to engage them. I think Torgerson met with these Apaches and sent Boggs to bribe them with a cow."

"Why?" Quist asked.

"Two reasons," Jock said. "One, Torgerson didn't want to lose a bunch of cattle to Apache raiders. Two, he wanted them to go after the X8 cattle. Boggs probably told them where we were and offered them even bigger rewards. Maybe even some help."

"You got it all figured out, have you, Kane?" Quist asked, a sarcastic snarl to his words.

"I know the Apaches didn't steal that cow. It was a gift, and Boggs was the messenger."

"Maybe," Quist said. "You don't have a hell of a lot of proof."

"I can put two and two together," Jock said. "And maybe I can come up with some more numbers to add in. Now, wear out some saddle leather and report back to me in two hours."

"What about Boggs?" Beeson asked. "Shouldn't we bury him?"

"I'll take care of Boggs," Jock said. "Now, get going. The Apache tracks should be easy to follow."

The men turned their horses. Quist led the scouts, who fanned out and followed. Jock watched them go, wondering how many of them he could trust. Morley was the one to watch. He had shot Boggs dead without hesitation—a man he knew. And Jock had a pretty good idea why Dub had killed Boggs: He was afraid Boggs would give him away, give up a secret about Morley that Dub didn't want known.

Jock's mind was swarming with suspicions. He knew he couldn't prove that Dub was in the pay of Torgerson, but things were beginning to add up that pointed in that direction. Torgerson would stop at nothing to beat Chad Becker into Ellsworth, even resorting to bribery of the Apaches. So, why wouldn't he also have a man in his service who was in Becker's camp?

Sooner or later, Jock thought, Dub would tip his hand, would give himself away. He had already shown that he was probably trying to delay the drive, and now he had killed a man, a man he had known well, just to keep Boggs's mouth shut.

As he caught up the dead man's horse, Jock knew he had to find a way to expose Dub.

The question was, he mused, was Dub the only one? Who else among the hands working for Becker might be in Torgerson's employ? One, or several?

Jock stood down from his horse and led Boggs's horse over to the dead body. He waited a few minutes, talking to the horse, a sorrel gelding, patting his neck and rubbing his withers.

"You hold steady, boy. You're going to carry your master back where he belongs."

The horse whickered softly in response to Jock's tone of voice.

After the horse settled down and stopped its wide-eyed inspection of Boggs, Jock reached down and picked up the body. It was starting to stiffen and it smelled of death and feces. He laid Boggs over the saddle, face-down, then unlashed his lariat. He hog-tied the dead man to the saddle, running the rope through the stirrups and wrapping it around him. He tightened the rope and tied it off beneath the horse.

Then Jock mounted his own horse while holding the reins of the other. He rode eastward toward where he figured Torgerson's herd would be.

"Let them bury the man," he said to himself.

Two hours later, the sorrel gelding whickered in recognition. Jock spotted the wranglers at the tail end of the herd, driving the extra horses. He reined up and pulled on the reins of the sorrel. Then he slapped it on the rump and watched it trot off toward the remuda. He turned his horse and rode away, back to the X8 herd.

"Torgerson will have something to talk about tonight at bed-down," Jock said to his own horse, then put the spurs to it and galloped off, knowing he had a long ride ahead.

Jock rode with even more determination than he'd had when he started the drive. He had not wanted to trail boss the X8 herd, but he needed the money. Now he had even more incentive to drive the herd to Ellsworth.

He wanted to beat Torgerson, make him sorry he had ever tried to cheat Chad by the foulest of means. Torgerson was now his enemy, as well as Chad's. And Jock meant to conquer Torgerson and hand Chad a victory when they reached Ellsworth ahead of the Cross J herd.

Chapter 16

Curt Torgerson seethed with murderous rage when he saw the body of Pip Boggs, still tied to the saddle of his horse. He glared at Chaco Vargas, the wrangler who had brought him the news. He stared daggers at Merle Fellows, the head wrangler, who held the sorrel's reins in his hand.

"Somebody's going to pay might dear for this," Torgerson said, his lips flared back from his teeth in a tiger's snarl, his fists bunching up like fleshy mallets. "Who in hell brought Pip in like this? Who in hell killed him?"

"We don't know, boss. That's for sure," Fellows said.

"You didn't see anybody? You mean the horse just trotted on back to you with Pip all tied up like a damned Christmas package?"

"No, sir," Fellows said, his voice just a tone or two above a respectful whisper. "Somebody trailed Pip up close and prodded his horse so's it run up on us. The feller was just too far away for us to see who it was."

"It wasn't an Apache, was it?"

"No, it was not an Apache," Vargas said. "The man looked like Jock Kane."

"Kane did this?"

Vargas shook his head. "I do not know."

"Chaco, you ride up to the tack wagon with Pip and get a shovel and you bury him. This herd is going to keep moving, no matter what." Torgerson's rage seemed to wither those around him. He rode off, leaving the men to wonder what their boss would do next. They were used to his boiling temper, but none had ever seen him so angry.

Torgerson had been driving the men and the herd mercilessly, said some, while others said it was better than sitting around whittling on a poor man's porch. He rode away from his foiled plan at a full gallop, whipping his palomino with his rein tips and raking his spurs into the animal's flanks until it quivered beneath him like a sack full of coiled springs, its muscles rippling, sweat oiling its hide to a high sheen.

There were two men Torgerson wanted to

talk to and he knew just where they were—where he had put them so that they could guard the left flank of the herd, near the tail end of it. If trouble was to come, that was where he figured it would come first. He had picked those men because he knew they would follow orders and shoot to kill if anyone threatened the herd or the drovers.

He caught up to Dan Fogarty first, spotting him in the sheets of dust that seemed to hang along the left flank of the herd. The drovers were pushing the cattle at his orders, pushing them hard off the grass, yelling each day until they were hoarse and working their horses into a frothy sweat that kept the wranglers busy changing mounts.

"Ho, D.F.," Torgerson called. "Hold up."

Fogarty turned his horse and stared in Torgerson's direction. A faded blue bandanna covered the lower part of his face, the cloth saturated with grit and dust, indented over the mouth from inhalation.

"Yo, Mr. Torgerson," Fogarty said as the two met.

"Where's Randy?" Torgerson asked.

"Oh, he's up yonder a ways, eating dust same as me."

"Let's catch up to him. I want to talk to you two boys."

Randy Clutter was the more dangerous of the two men, the more aggressive. Torgerson had kept the two men away from Abel Kane on purpose. Kane rode up in front, as a kind of secondary point man, where Torgerson could keep an eye on him. He thought of Abel as being on a kind of probation until Torgerson could see how he handled trouble and followed orders. Clutter and Fogarty were born hardcases, and both had reputations decidedly on the unsavory side. They might not have notches on the butts of their pistols, but everyone knew they had killed men before and were always one step ahead of the law.

"What's on your mind, Mr. Torgerson?" Fogarty asked.

"I got a job for you two boys."

"We can do most anything you want."

"I'm counting on it," Torgerson said as they rode on through the strong smells of cattle and the gritty veils of dust.

D.F. was one of those callow young men whose family had been broken up by the war. His father was killed at Corinth, and his mother had taken up with his uncle and several other men who had not gone to war, leaving Dan feeling abandoned and neglected. He had gotten into an argument with his uncle, Jesse Fogarty, and had shot him dead. His mother backed his claim of self-defense and D.F. had gotten out of that scrape. But the young man had found killing to his liking. He probably felt the government owed him something because they had taken away his father and made his mother into a whore. So he took to the owlhoot trail, along with his friend, an orphan kid whose parents had both been killed, and whose older sister had been abducted by Comanches during the war.

Randy was an entirely different breed, however, than the likes of Dan Fogarty. Randy was smart, wise as a cur dog who knew how to rob and steal without getting seen or caught, and he had perfected his skills over time so that he always had money and food. But Torgerson knew Randy longed to be accepted by society, and while he taught D.F. and Abel Kane how to rob and steal, he secretly wished to earn a living as a rancher. When Torgerson caught him rustling cattle some years before, he had given the young man a piece of advice when turning him loose without hanging him or calling the law down on him.

"If you ever want to join the society that cast you out, son, you come and see me. I'll give you a job and teach you how to raise cows so you won't never have to steal none ever again."

Apparently the advice had stuck because Randy now worked for him, and he had brought two good men with him, Abel Kane and Dan Fogarty. But Torgerson hadn't hired him out of altruism, or any generosity connected with human kindness. He had hired Randy because of his larcenous past, just for this drive, because he wanted to beat Chad Becker and pursue his own path toward personal wealth. Torgerson, in a moment of self-examination, realized that he and Randy were both cut out of the same bolt. If Torgerson had been orphaned, he might have followed the same path as Clutter. But Torgerson had grown up with money. His father was a horse thief, and a good one, and when he was finally caught and hanged for his crimes, he left his family with two invaluable assets: land and money.

Before he died, Olaf Torgerson had told his son that he stole horses for the thrill of it. "But I also wanted you and your mother to be proud people, to own land and to acquire monetary wealth. You've got the means, son; now make it count."

Torgerson had followed that advice, but he

had also realized that, in the process of acquiring land and wealth, a man who had scruples was definitely handicapped. There were a lot of ways to steal, he had learned, which were not strictly against the law. To Curt Torgerson, money was power, and with power a man could steal without ever getting his hands too dirty.

"I made money from nothing," Olaf had told his son. "I sold horses to the army during the war. They never asked where I got them and I never told them. That was making money out of nothing, like picking wild grapes and making wine. But when you have money, that money can be used to beget more money. Down the line, nobody will ever ask you where you got your money. They won't care. Money makes more friends than it does enemies. Money begets money. So that's what I leave you, Curt. Money and land. They are your tools. Grow food on the land and people will give you more money. The more money you have the more land you can buy. The more land you have, the more things you can grow, whether it be cattle or cotton or corn."

Torgerson never forgot his father's words, and he remembered them now as he formed a plan in his mind—a plan that would add to his wealth while keeping his own hands clean. With money, he could hire people who would dirty their hands while his remained clean. It was as simple as that, in Torgerson's raging mind.

"What is it you want us to do, Mr. Torgerson?" Clutter asked.

"Let's ride off farther from the herd so we can be by ourselves," Torgerson said.

The two young men followed Torgerson. He rode some distance from the herd, even though there was nobody near enough to hear them over the lowing of the cattle and the faint rumble they made as the drovers pushed them ever northward.

When Torgerson reined up, the other two crowded their horses in close, eager to hear what he had to say. Torgerson could tell that they were proud to be singled out for a private conversation.

"D.F., Randy, I've been keeping an eye on you two boys, and you make fine hands. But I've got a job for you that carries a lot more responsibility, and maybe some risk. Interested?"

Randy and D.F. nodded.

"I know you two are tight with Abel Kane, but I don't want him to know anything about this just now. That all right with you?"

"We don't tell Abel everything we do," Clutter said.

"No, sir," D.F. said.

"Good. Because I'm going to make you two my bounty hunters. Do you know what that is?"

Both Clutter and Fogarty shook their heads.

"You got to be real good at this, but I think you two can handle the job all right. I'm going to pay you five dollars apiece extra for every X8 hand you bring down. How's that sound to you?"

"What do you mean 'bring down?' " Clutter asked.

"I want you to use your long rifles and shoot Becker's drovers. Pick them off one by one, without getting caught."

"Oh boy," D.F. said, his words more expressive of shock than pleasure.

"That don't seem like much for such a job, Mr. Torgerson," Clutter said. "A man's life ought to be worth more than five dollars. A sawbuck would sound a lot better to me."

Torgerson smiled. He knew he had them.

"All right, Randy. Ten bucks for each X8 cowpoke you shoot."

"You want us to kill them, right?" D.F. said.

Torgerson didn't answer. Clutter looked at his friend and shook his head in disbelief.

"Yeah, D.F., he wants us to put their lamps out."

"Oh, sure," Fogarty said.

"I'll need proof," Torgerson said.

"Scalps?" Clutter asked, deadly serious.

"No, of course not," Torgerson said. "Just something that let's me know you did your job."

"How about we bring you their shirts with a bullet hole and some blood on them? That do it?" Clutter said.

Torgerson nodded. "Yep, that would do it," he said. "I'll give you ten dollars a shirt."

Clutter grinned. "When do you want us to start?" he asked.

"You got plenty of ammunition for those long rifles?"

"We got enough," D.F. said. "And we're both damned good shots."

"Then you two drift off by yourselves, head south. Find that X8 herd and start work. Don't come back for a week. When you do and you bring me those shirts, I'll pay you on the spot."

"Oh, boy," D.F. said, this time, with glee.

"And if you want to earn extra money, boys," Torgerson said, "you bring me the shirt and hat of Jock Kane and I'll pay you fifty dollars for them. I'll pay you fifty dollars for the shirt and hat of Chad Becker, too."

Clutter grinned and stuck out his hand. Torgerson took it.

"Stop by the chuck wagon and draw yourselves some grub. Tell Cookie you're going hunting," Torgerson said.

"You got yourself two bounty hunters, Mr. Torgerson," Clutter said. "See you in a week."

Torgerson smiled as the two men rode off to the south.

"That ought to slow Chad up," he said to himself, without the slightest twinge of conscience.

Chapter 17

The wind began with a whisper.

The grasses trembled as faint zephyrs jostled them. A meadowlark on a mesquite bush huddled as fingers of air rustled its back and wing feathers, and still it sat on the branch, blinking its yellow-brown eyes. Little tendrils of dust spooled up in miniature whirlwinds in a wallow where quail were preening their wings like feathered bathers learning to swim. Calico Sal, the lead cow in the X8 herd, lifted her boss and swung her horns as her nostrils flexed like rubbery diaphragms to pick up any alien or intrusive scent.

The sun had slid over the horizon, gilding the western clouds, bleaching the edges of the larger ones to a silver sheen before rusting the thin ones close to the earth, turning them golden in some kind of mysterious alchemy. The sky that morning had been drenched in blood, so scarlet that it lingered in Jock's retinas long after it evaporated into a moil of gray cloud clusters.

Now, Jock looked at Calico Sal and at the gigantic quilt of the herd as it billowed and flowed over the dusking land, headed for the water he had found a mile or two ahead. Their mottled bodies surged as a single tide, their horns like white-capped ripples in a sea of light and shadow, bobbing colors smeared on rolling combers.

Jock looked to the west and felt dismay as the sky began to darken and he saw the elephantine clouds blowing toward them. He looked up and saw the big white thunderheads sailing across the dissolving blue of the sky like galleons and caravels pushed by a trade wind from some far-off region of a darkening sea.

"Red sky at morning, sailor take warning," Jock intoned, thinking of that crimson sky at dawn. "Red sky at night, sailor's delight."

But there was no red sky that afternoon and the western sky was already blackening with ominous thunderheads. He turned his horse and rode back until he spotted Dewey Ringler, who had been riding point. Dewey was now ordering the hands to bunch the herd up behind Calico Sal, perhaps sensing that the cattle were getting as jumpy as Sal.

Jock gestured to Dewey, beckoning to him so that he would ride over and they could talk.

Ringler barked orders to the drovers and wove his way through the stream of cows until he was in the clear.

"What's up, Jock?"

"I see you've got a handle on this spooky herd," Jock said. "One clap of thunder might throw them into a panic."

"I can smell something," Ringler said, "something I don't like to smell."

Jock turned his head to the west, sniffed at the tug of breeze that seemed to be rising above the ground. The smell was faint, but it was there.

"Dust?" Jock said.

"See them high clouds? That's a high wind pushing them across the sky. We can't see it yet, but there's something behind that blowing up yonder. I'd say we're in for a hell of a storm."

"A rainstorm?"

Jock turned his horse out of the wind and pulled the makings from his pocket. While Ringler talked, Jock rolled a cigarette, perhaps knowing it might be his last chance for a while.

"Maybe not rain right off," Ringler said. "Something a hell of a lot worse."

Ringler paused while Jock lit his cigarette. The match blew out as soon as Jock uncapped his hand and exposed it to the air.

"Looks like a dust storm to me," Ringler said.

Jock shuddered inwardly. He had been in dust storms before. He remembered, as a child, when his mother had hung wet blankets over the windows to keep the dust from blowing into the house. When they took them down, they weighed a ton, and the house was filled with fine dust that took weeks to sweep out from every corner.

"That could be bad," Jock said. "We'll lose some head."

"It's like drowning in dirt," Ringler said.

Chad rode up, his eyes wide with alarm.

"Jock," Becker said, "it don't look good."

"Ringler thinks we're in for a dust storm."

"Oh, God." Chad wet his lips as if to ward off the coming dryness.

"The San Antonio River is just ahead," Ringler said. "We could bed the herd down somewhere near Goliad. String them out all along it. Maybe the river will take their minds off the blowing dust."

Jock shook his head as he puffed on his dangling cigarette. Smoke spewed from his mouth and nostrils.

"If we get a dust storm, we could also get rain right behind it. We'll water the cattle and move the herd past the river. I don't want to get caught in a flash flood."

"God, no," Chad said.

"It's going to be a long night," Jock said. "Water them, then push on beyond the river another three miles or so."

"It'll be a job," Ringler said.

"Let's get to it. I look for those scouts to come in if they've got any sense at all. Keep an eye out for them."

"You're not worried about Apaches?" Chad asked.

"They read weather better than we do," Jock said. "They'll hole up somewhere until this blow is over."

Chad nodded with the eagerness of hope.

The wind picked up a short time later as the sky turned to ashes in the west and the black clouds mushroomed in size, blowing their way. The sky turned to carbon, and the wind began to whip at the herd and the men with savage gusts. Then there was a momentary pause, as if the earth was holding its breath. The cattle moved on to the river and fanned out. Drovers began searching for fords in the darkness. Many cut mesquite branches and trimmed them into long poles. They used these to test the bottom and, when they found the fords, they drove the cattle across in small bunches, the animals groaning and protesting until the din rose to a high pitch and men had to shout to be heard.

The dry, musty smell of the cattle changed to a clinging, wet aroma of musk as the herd crossed the San Antonio River in pitch darkness. Jock had some of the men light torches, after dipping mesquite branches in coal oil. The torches, he told them, would serve as a beacon to the scouts. The wind whipped at the flames until they flapped like beaten rugs on a clothesline.

Horky and his men were the first to ride up and find Jock, who was now riding swing to keep the herd from straying too far to the west after they crossed the river. Jock was eager to see him.

"We did not see any Apaches," Horky said.

"I didn't expect you would." Jock's cigarette had gone out long before, and he knew he could not smoke in that wind. The dust was now stinging his face and scouring his clothes, becoming embedded in the fibers of his shirt and trousers. He held his head down to keep the dust from blowing up his nose.

"But we did see two men riding this way," Horky said. "When they saw us, they pulled their rifles out. I think they were going to shoot at us."

"What made you think that?"

Beeson crowded his horse in close as if he wanted to say something. Jock could barely see him through the dust and the inky blackness of the night.

"Horky's right," Beeson said. "They cocked them rifles soon as they plucked 'em from their scabbards. They was hunters, Jock."

"Hunters? What do you mean?"

"They were damned sure looking for something to shoot. We lit a shuck and hightailed it out of there, but I heard them levers on their rifles squeak loud as a pair of barn doors swinging open."

"Do you know who they were, Horky?" Jock asked.

Horky shook his head. "I never see them before."

"Beeson?"

"Nope. Young fellers, they were."

"Did you get a good look at them? Either

of you?" Jock looked closely at each man, putting his face close to theirs.

"No time," Beeson said. "But they looked like a couple of hardcases to me."

"Horky?"

"They were too far away," he said.

"What about their horses?" Jock asked. "Did you get a good look at their horses?"

"One of 'em was riding a claybank mare," Beeson said. "The other was on a dun gelding. Five- or six-year-olds, I'd say."

A klaxon warning sounded in Jock's brain. "They look like cow ponies to you, Beeson? Small, chunky horses, maybe fourteen or fifteen hands high?"

"Yeah, I'd say."

"The claybank," Jock said. "Cropped mane?"

"Yeah, come to think of it," Beeson said. "Bobbed mane and tail."

"That is true," Horky said. "And the dun, it had a black mane and tail."

Jock didn't say anything right away.

"Do you know those jaspers?" Beeson asked Jock.

"I don't know them," Jock said. "But I think I know who they are."

He wasn't going to tell Horky and Beeson, but he knew that those were the two men his brother Abel had been associating with for the past several months. Both were troublemakers, ne'er-do-wells, always in hot water with the law.

"Randy Clutter and D.F. Fogarty. I think Fogarty's name is Dan, but he goes by D.F." Jock spoke aloud, not expecting a reaction. But Beeson spoke up.

"I heard of them two, all right," he said. "Cattle rustlers, horse thieves."

"Maybe even killers," Jock said.

"I think those two wanted to kill us," Horky said. "That is the way they acted."

"I think so, too," Beeson said. "You can tell."

"How's that, Amos?" Jock asked.

"First off, they didn't act like they was on the run. They was riding toward our herd. Like they had a purpose, you know? And when they spotted us, they didn't try to run or hide. They just kept coming on and pulled them rifles from their boots. I think they was hunting X8 men and knew who the hell we all were."

"What about you, Horky?" Jock asked. "That the way you see it?"

Horcasitas nodded with a vigorous movement of his head. "Yes, I think Amos is right. That is how they looked. Like hunters. Hunters of men. They wanted to kill us. I had the feeling in my stomach that these men were going to kill us. If we do not run away, they shoot us."

"Chad told me my brother was with those two," Jock said. "And he said that Abel is working for Torgerson, driving the Cross J herd up to Ellsworth. You didn't see another man did you? My brother?"

Both men shook their heads.

"Well, nothing we can do about it now," Jock said. "You were lucky. I'm glad you didn't get into a fight with those two."

"What do you make of it, Jock?" Beeson asked.

"I think Torgerson sent those two down here to pick us off, Amos. Pick us off one by one."

Beeson swore. "Then we got big trouble," he said.

"Yeah, we do. But nothing we can't handle. You keep a sharp eye out, all of you. Let's see if we can't pick those two off before they spill any X8 blood."

The wind picked up then, and it seemed like a sheet of sand rose up and enveloped them. There was a wolfish howl to it, and grit stung their faces and blinded them, turned them into voiceless mutes. In seconds, none of the men could see their own hands in front of their faces.

And the X8 cattle began to bawl. To Jock they sounded like the voices of lost souls screaming from the depths of hell.

Chapter 18

Jock slipped his bandanna from his neck, wet it down with water from his canteen, then tied it over his face like a mask. Still, he could barely breathe as the air filled with dust. His eyes stung as if salted, and his lungs burned with the effort to breathe.

The cattle were suffering, he knew. The ones on the western fringes of the herd caught the brunt of the wind, but the dust was everywhere, and the cattle moaned and groaned, bellowing and roaring, like beasts in a slaughter pen. He and the drovers did their best to keep them from stampeding, and the dust and darkness probably helped. The cattle could not see where to run, so they stayed huddled together in the herd.

Chad rode nearby and, suddenly, Jock saw

his boss double over in the saddle, rip off his bandanna, and begin to retch. The sound was more horrible than the wind, than the bellowing roars of the cattle. Jock put a hand on Chad's shoulder, finding it in the darkness by some unexplained miracle, it seemed to him.

"Chad, what's wrong?"

More coughing and horrible retching. Jock could hear something come up through Chad's throat, tearing tissue as it rumbled from some dark and sour place deep inside him. Chad leaned over and vomited onto the ground. A rider rode up out of the heavy mist of dust, bearing a torch that sputtered and whished like some angry whisperer, its flames leaping to escape the oil-soaked branch.

"You got some trouble here?" Earl Foster asked. Jock barely recognized the man. The voice helped him with his identification.

"I don't know, Earl. Stay with us a while."

Foster nodded, ducking his head as if to avoid the wind.

It was then that Jock saw flecks of red on Chad's shirt, and when he erupted again, bright splotches of blood spewed forth, mingled with black bile from his stomach.

"Chad," Jock said, tightening his fingers into talons on the man's shoulder.

Chad waved an arm in the air as if to ward

off Jock's words or drive him away. He gulped in air, fighting for his breath.

"Medicine," Chad gasped. "Pocket. Shirt pocket."

Jock patted the front of Chad's shirt with his left hand and felt a bulging glass shape in one pocket. He reached in and pulled the bottle out. He jerked the cork, then shielded the opening from the lashing dust.

"It's open, Chad." Jock handed him the bottle.

Chad straightened up and swallowed a gulp of the murky brown medicine, then handed the bottle back to Jock. Jock corked it and replaced it in Chad's pocket.

"What's wrong with you, Chad? You see a doc about this?"

Chad nodded, still unable to speak. He tied the bandanna on and pulled it tight to his chin. Jock could hear him wheezing beneath it.

"Ulcers, I think," Chad croaked.

"Ulcers? Stomach ulcers?"

"That's what Doc Fordyce thinks." Chad's voice was a loud, raspy whisper close to Jock's ear.

"Fargo? In Corpus?"

"Yeah, Ford Fargo. He gave me that medicine."

"He's a quack," Jock said. "And a drunk."

"He's a good medico, Jock. He delivered my daughter. My wife, Rachael, swears by him. She made me go."

Jock knew Fordyce Fargo from the visits he made to treat Jock's mother when she had the fever. He knew him by his whiskey breath and his rumpled clothing, his soiled shirts and his bedraggled mustache. But he also knew that Fargo's hands, especially his fingernails, were always clean, as if he continually washed them in lye soap and scalding water. He supposed Fargo had been a good enough doctor when he was a young man, but the years of drinking and carousing with immoral women had taken their toll on the physician. When Jock had last seen him, he had been repulsed by the man, and by the reek of alcohol that was like a cloak around his unkempt person. He had heard a story in Corpus Christi about Fargo and his wife, Livia. Apparently Livia disapproved of her husband's drinking, and wouldn't let him bring John Barleycorn into the house. So Fordyce would camp out with his drinking cronies and they'd all sit around the fire and swap lies, getting blind drunk. When Fordyce went back home, he told his wife that he had been on a house call. She saw through this, though, and always remarked to him, "I know you've been to the campfire, Ford, so take a bath and sober up before you come to bed in my house."

Ford Fargo's campfire had become quite a legend in that part of Texas. Now, whenever a cowhand was out at night and saw a campfire, he'd say, "I wonder if Ford Fargo is a-settin' there, a-passin' the whiskey bottle."

"How much of that stuff have you got?" Jock asked.

"Two cases," Chad said. "Jubilee's packing it in the chuck wagon."

"You ought to go back home, Chad. Go back to Rachael and your daughter, Victoria. They can take care of you. You're spitting up blood."

"Yeah, I know. I'm not going back home, Jock. I'm riding all the way to Ellsworth with this herd."

"Your wife know about this?" Jock asked, with a sudden stab of intuition.

Chad hesitated, then finally shook his head.

"Well, before we get to the Red, everybody in the outfit will know about it. Go on back home. I can take the herd to Kansas."

"Jocko, let it go. I'm going all the way. I can ride this out."

"All right, Chad. Suit yourself. But if you

become crippled, or get in my way, I'll send you back home if I have to hogtie you."

"You won't have to worry about me."

Chad's words rang false on Jock's ears, but he nodded and clapped his friend on the back, then rode ahead, the horse balking at every step. Chad followed, gasping and choking on the dust, the sounds muffled in the blowing wind.

One by one the torches blew out, and Jock knew there was no way any of the men could light them again. The darkness was almost total, and the wind did not lessen.

Jock fought his way along the edge of the herd, the sand stinging his face, arms and legs. He knew the horse must be suffering intolerably, and the cattle were protesting with loud bellows and moaning growls.

Out of the darkness, a rider appeared, a shadow on horseback, looking like some phantom risen from the ground itself.

"Captain, it's me, Ed Purvis."

"Good. You got back, all of you?"

"I seen Quist, so he's come back, and we all did. Been at the leading edge of the herd, and Naylor says they're trying to turn east, keep the wind at their rumps."

"We've got to hold them to the north line," Jock said.

"Naylor told me to come find you. We need help. Calico Sal keeps turning right. The cattle are following her."

"How far?" Jock asked.

"Maybe a quarter mile or more."

"All right. Tell Fred we're coming."

"Hell, I don't know if I can find my way back," Purvis said.

"Then stick with us. You probably can't get there any sooner than us in this wind."

"I'll lead us back," Purvis said. "It's just hard going is all."

Chad, Jock and Purvis rode on, the wind blasting them with sand and grit, the air thick with fine dust. Jock could barely see the cattle off to his right. He heard them and put together the image of them blindly walking, packed together. Maybe, he thought, the cattle had it better, some of them. They could hold their heads down and breathe better than he could.

Finally, Purvis slowed and turned his horse. He beckoned to Jock and Chad. They followed him until more riders appeared, phantasms without faces or eyes, dust-covered as if they had risen from graves.

"Cap'n Jock," Naylor said, riding up close. Jock didn't recognize him at all.

"Yeah. Having a time of it, are you?"

"That damned Sal keeps running off to the east. I've got men on the other side beating them back, but they all want to put this wind at their backs and I don't think we can do a hell of a lot about it."

Naylor was almost shouting, but his words sounded as if they were spoken through cotton batting and Jock had to strain to understand him.

"Well, we can put a rope on Sal," Jock said. "But I'm not going to do that."

"There's one steer that's trying its best to kill some of us. He keeps at Sal's heels and I think he's pushing her."

"Take me over there, Fred," Jock yelled.

Calico Sal was surrounded by three cowhands, all trying to turn her back. They were waving their arms and yelling at Sal, but she was smart. She'd start one way and then quickly change course, always presenting her hind end to the sandpaper wind.

Jock rode up to one of the hands and told him to stop trying to turn Sal.

"Let her stay where she is," Jock said. "We'll let the herd bunch up here and bed down for the night."

"Sure, boss," the hand said, and Jock recognized him as Vic Cussler. Dewey Ringler was there, too, along with a young hand named Cory Wingate. They all looked exhausted.

"It's not Sal I'm worried about," Cussler said. "Watch yourself, Jock."

Out of the corner of his eye, Jock saw a dark shape moving out of the pack, its huge horns ticking with pelting sand. The steer charged straight at Jock, bellowing with a deep, chesty roar, its head lowered and its tail switching like a puma's.

"Here he comes again," Ringler shouted. He spurred his horse to try to head the steer off. Jock dug spurs into his horse's flanks and felt the animal bunch up its muscles and bound into the air. The sweeping horns, all six feet of them, narrowly missed the horse's left flank. But the steer swung its head as Ringler approached and one tip caught him in the leg, shoving his boot out of the stirrup.

Ringler threw up his hands as if trying to grab a ladder in the air. Instead, his horse bucked as the horn raked its left hind flank and Ringler ejected out of the saddle like a jack-in-the-box at the end of a coiled spring. He hit the ground hard as Naylor leaped from his horse and bulldogged the steer, clasping its horns on both sides and hanging on for dear life.

The steer shook its head and bucked like a

horse, swinging around and pawing the ground to shreds with its cloven hooves. Naylor went flying and the steer shook its brute shoulders, looking around for another target.

Jock rode up on his horse and diverted the steer, then rode circles around it until it wore itself out and stood there, panting and snorting, coughing on sand.

"You got him stopped, Jock," Ringler shouted as he stood up and patted his pants, as if that would get rid of the dirt and dust.

"I wonder," Jock said to the men gathered around him, "if whoever cut that steer has still got both balls."

The men didn't laugh, but turned their backs to the wind as the cattle herd came to a stop and milled around until their rumps faced west, into the brunt of the ferocious, dust-laden wind that ripped at them like a billion sharp-toothed insects sawing at their hides with tiny razors.

Jock spit out sand and wiped granules from his lips. He was dying for a cigarette.

Chapter 19

Torgerson watched the tangle of cattle swarming in circles just before the first one slid off the hardpan and disappeared into a deep hole, where the current caught it and funneled the animal downstream. The other cattle dropped off the shelf one by one and, after being dunked into the same hole, were swept away by the rapid current. He saw these things happen through a curtain of blinding dust and then watched as more cattle clomped into the narrow ford, struggled for their footing and then slid off to flounder downstream, bawling and gasping for air.

"Eddie, Jack," Torgerson called out. He was looking toward two riders he could barely see in the gloom of late afternoon. They were the nearest drovers. "Come here, quick."

He felt as if his words were being swallowed up by the cloud of dust and blown back into his mouth by the wind. But the men heard him, evidently, because they turned their horses away from the slowly streaming column of cattle drifting down to the San Antonio River crossing.

The two men bent over their horses' necks like masked mendicants, their bandannas besmirched with sweat and dirt, their eyes thin slits flocked with grains of grit. Ed Timmons and Jack Colvin were two hands who had been with the Cross J and Torgerson since before the war. Two men he trusted, as much as he trusted any men—hard workers, good hands, loyal to a proverbial fault.

"Yeah, Curt," Eddie said. "We got our hands plumb full."

"No, look down there," Torgerson shouted. "This is a bad ford."

"Holy shit," Eddie said, his words muffled through the bandanna.

Jack rode up for a look, craning his neck to see through the brown haze.

"Damn that Cobb," Jack said.

Rufus Cobb was the man who had picked out that particular ford. Jack looked around as if to skewer the man with a dirty look, a look that he could not have delivered even if Cobb had been two feet away.

"Rufus is on the other side," Torgerson said, as if reading Jack's mind. "I sent him over with the first bunch."

"We got to cut this bunch back," Eddie said. "Those cows will drown for sure."

"I'll help you," Torgerson said, rifling his voice through the curtain of sand and wind by cupping his hands into a megaphone.

The three men turned into the herd and took off their hats. They slapped at cows, bulling them with their horses to turn away from the river. They batted at their eyes and cursed at them with a rage born of fear and necessity. The cattle fought back, swinging their horns and bawling in protest, much like a human mob being turned away from a free lunch at a local tavern.

Gradually, the herd began to turn. The three men pressed the leaders back into the herd, jamming them into those cattle that wanted to continue forward, those with the smell of water in their nostrils and panic in their hearts to escape the dust.

Abel Kane rode up and joined in with the others to continue turning the herd back in on itself. It was a treacherous, muscle-straining task, made even more dangerous by the profusion of sharp horns twisting and jabbing so close to the flanks of the horses and the legs of the men. In fact, some of the cattle drew blood from Eddie and Jack's legs, the tips of their horns raking their legs just above their boots, since they were burrowed so deep in the herd. The two men kicked at the encroaching cows, striking them on their bosses so hard that the animals backed up and helped clog the leading edge of the riverbound herd.

Abel forced his way into the herd, making a wedgelike opening that allowed Eddie and Jack to escape being crushed by animals determined to forge ahead of their leaders and make it to the water.

Eddie wove his horse through the narrow opening and stepped clear of the milling cattle. Jack was not so lucky. As he tried to follow Eddie out, one of the longhorns raised its head as Jack's horse brushed past it, then lowered its massive boss. None of the men saw the steer's head again until it rose up and swung left, then right. The cattle nearby moaned and grunted, then fell back against one another to get out of the way of the lethal horns. The steer charged straight at Jack's horse, rising up off its forelegs with each forward lunge. Jack heard the commotion and turned to see what was happening. He was too late.

The steer, bellowing and roaring, lowered his head again, then thrust upward with one horn. The tip caught Jack's horse in the left flank. The steer twisted its head with a sudden, violent movement and, still charging, ripped through the bowels of the horse.

The horse screamed in agony as its intestines fell like a sack of lead through a trap door on a gallows, and staggered to one side. The steer's horn continued its deadly path and ripped into the horse's rib cage, piercing a lung. The horse's legs collapsed at the knees and it went down.

Jack fought his left stirrup with his boot, trying to extricate himself. He kicked out of the right stirrup, which left him off balance. As the horse fell on its right side, Jack, his left foot still caught in the stirrup, slid out of the saddle and tumbled downward, pitching face forward onto the rump of the savage steer.

Jack's yell was cut short when he bounced off the steer and struck the ground. The fall knocked the breath from his lungs, and then the rampaging steer kicked both hind legs into the air. Its hooves smashed into Jack, one landing on the side of his head, the other ripping into his shoulder, shearing through his shirt and plowing a furrow into his flesh, leaving a raw, bloody wound. Jack swooned, his senses scrambled by the blow to his head. In seconds, the other cattle streamed over him, hooves slashing and pounding at his limp body.

Abel watched through the brown scrim of dust and rammed his spurs into his horse's flanks, causing the animal to bound forward into the onrushing tide of cattle that were burying Jack alive. He shouted into the wind, and started kicking at the cattle to drive them back and away, but they bulled forward, the blood smell strong in their nostrils, their fear blazing like candles in their distended brown eyes. The noise of their bellowing was deafening. Abel saw Jack lying there, inert, seemingly lifeless, and he leaned over in an attempt to reach him, to pull him from the ground. But his reach was far too short and his horse was being pummeled by horns and heads. It backed away from the sheer crushing force of the wild-eyed cattle surging en masse to either escape or attack whatever was in their path.

Abel wrestled with his frightened horse. He kicked at the heads of cattle to drive them away from the fallen Jack. The cattle nearest him turned, choking off some of the surge.

They trampled the dead horse, however, and the smell of blood threw those cattle into an even wilder panic. But they streamed past Abel and turned again toward the river.

"Kane," Torgerson yelled, "get the hell out of there."

"Come on, Abel," Eddie pleaded. "You're making it worse."

"Jack," Abel yelled through his bandanna. That was the only word he could get out as he struggled to keep his horse from rearing or kicking at cattle with its hind legs. It was like riding a whirlwind, and his ears filled with the sounds of bawling cattle, the dust-laden wind and the shouts of the men trying to turn the outlaw cattle away from the treacherous river ford.

Abel jerked hard on the reins, pulling his horse's head downward, bowing his neck. Then he slid slowly from the saddle, still holding hard to the reins and stood beside Jack. He reached down as he bent over to shorten the distance of his reach, and slid a hand under Jack's left arm. With a mighty effort, he tugged Jack up and then wrapped his arm around the man's chest. Still grasping the reins, he got his weight beneath Jack and heaved him onto the back of his horse. The horse tried to move away from this unwelcome weight, but cattle blocked it from sidling out from under Jack's limp body.

Abel pushed Jack so that he bent like a horseshoe over the horse's hind end. But his weight was balanced and when Abel was sure he would not slide off, he stuck a boot into the stirrup and, grabbing the saddle horn, hefted himself back into the saddle. He eased up on the reins. His horse snorted and bobbed its head as the bit cutting into the tender back of its mouth slid loose and eased the pain.

Jack turned the horse in a tight circle. He leaned back and pushed down on Jack's back with one hand so that he would not fall off. The horse lifted its rump and let fly with both hind legs, his hooves striking a longhorn in the side. Then Jack put his spurs to its flanks and the horse bolted from a standing position into a bound that carried it away from the thick clot of cattle at its heels.

The horse pushed past the bunched cattle in front of it, squeezing itself through the milling pack and headed for open ground where Torgerson and Eddie sat gape-mouthed atop their horses, their hat brims flapping in the wind, their bandannas billowing out at their necks. Jack nearly slid off Abel's horse, but Abel pressed harder on his back and he stayed on, still unconscious, but breathing.

His hat had been knocked off and was now a shredded tatter of felt on the ground, kicked hither and yon by the cattle until it lost all recognizable shape.

Eddie rode in close and put a hand on Jack so that Abel could ease up. Abel's arm ached from the strain and he shook it to restore circulation to the muscles.

"Let me drag Jack off and get him someplace we can give him some help," Eddie said. "You're lucky you didn't get gored or chewed up by them cattle."

Abel was out of breath. He only nodded. Torgerson helped Eddie pull Jack off of Abel's horse, and they held the injured man under his arms and rode away as if they had been doing such rescue work all their lives. Abel followed, glad to be away from the moil of cattle and those deadly horns and hooves.

"Drop him," Torgerson told Eddie. He let Jack's arm slip from his grip and Eddie was holding a lopsided weight.

Eddie could not hold Jack's weight by himself, so he had to watch as his own grip failed. Jack fell to the ground in a crumpled heap, like some tossed-away, oversized doll.

"Damn," Abel said and rode over.

Eddie looked at Torgerson as if to question his boss's decision.

"Get some more men up here, Eddie, and get these cows to a better crossing."

"Yes, sir," Eddie said, and made his way through the wind and dust to call in helpers to aid him in his task.

Abel swung down and lifted Jack up as he squatted down. Jack's head hung at a crazy angle, and he did not respond. Abel leaned in close to the man's mouth and listened. He heard a terrible wheezing sound and a kind of gurgling rattle. He peered at Jack's neck and saw that it was sunken and bruised. Even in the dim light, he could see that Jack's throat had been crushed.

Jack gave out a rattling sigh and made no more sound.

Torgerson looked down at the two men.

"He's dead, isn't he, Kane?"

"Yes, he's dead."

"You were a fool to risk your own life to save that poor man, Kane."

"Hell, he'd have done the same for me."

"No, he wouldn't have. I taught him better."

"What? What the hell do you mean, Mr. Torgerson?"

"I mean," Torgerson said, "that his death was written down in the book."

"What book?"

"The book of life, son. You can't change that book no matter how hard you try. Jack knew he was a dead man the minute he got off his horse. Best thing you could have done for him was shoot him dead the minute he hit the ground. So he wouldn't suffer."

"I, I . . . damned if I believe that, Mr. Torgerson."

"Then, you are a fool, Kane. And you'll die a fool. Now leave Jack's corpse be and get back to work."

Abel looked up at Torgerson, his eyes blazing with a deep hatred. Torgerson turned his horse and rode away, back toward the straying herd.

"You sonofabitch," Abel breathed, and the wind snatched away his whisper and blew it to pieces before it ever reached another human's ear. Abel clenched his fists and felt the seep of hot tears spill onto his dust-encrusted cheeks.

Chapter 20

Haggard, red-eyed men emerged from the long night like bewildered escapees from an asylum. They rousted the X8 cattle from their beds, somnambulists in slow motion, waders in a dust-filled sea, bucking the current of wind as they slouched in their saddles. Cattle arose from the ground and shook off the dust and dirt, glared at the murky world of morning and sought out their leaders, their stricken companions. The lowing began almost immediately and rippled through the herd until its chorus rose up into the brown sky like a lament.

"Wind is dying down," Chad croaked. His voice was hoarse from his vomiting during the night, and was no more than a raspy whisper.

"At least the cattle didn't stampede." Jock was trying to roll a cigarette, holding the paper and tobacco near his armpit, out of the wind. It was like trying to nail jelly to a wall. He was using just one hand, as usual, but the wind seemed to have fingers, and it sought the delicate paper and the brown shreds of tobacco. Somehow he managed to fold the paper around its cargo. He squeezed the quirly tight, twisted both ends, then licked the folded edge so that it stuck. He put the cigarette in his mouth, then wondered if he would ever get it lit.

"They're moving pretty well this morning," Chad said as he looked at Calico Sal at the head of the herd, her followers fanned out and streaming behind her.

"Chad, ride over to my windward side, will you? I want to try and light this stick in my mouth. Maybe you can lean over to block the wind."

The two men reined up and Chad maneuvered his horse, then leaned over while Jock cupped his hands and struck a match. A second later, a coil of smoke arose from the tobacco and Jock inhaled.

"What would you do without me, Jock?" Chad said.

"I wouldn't have this first smoke of the morning, that's for sure."

To the west, the pall of dust seemed to hang in the air, while near them they could see it moving like a toxic cloud, turning transparent in the blaze of the sunrise.

Later that day, Jock saw the destruction and now knew the source of the wind that was already subsiding as the dark clouds disappeared and broke up. In their path there was a wide swath of grassless ground that was littered with broken tree limbs, mangled ovals of prickly pear, limp, dead remnants of wildflowers, and bits of cloth and rope carried from some faraway place.

"A twister plowed through here," Jock said to Chad. "Probably hit some poor rancher first."

"What a mess. It would have played hob with the cattle if it had hit us during the night."

"The cattle and us."

Jock had sent the scouts out after he was satisfied that the herd was settled down and they were making good time across the plain.

"One of you—I don't care who—ride east and check on the Cross J bunch. I want to know if we're ahead of or behind them. Any volunteers?"

"I'll go," Beeson said.

Jock nodded. "Report back when you know, Amos," he said.

They made fifteen miles that day, and found a good place to bed down the cattle late in the afternoon.

"Fifteen thousand head sure do tear up the country," Jock said when he and Chad were alone after supper, a few yards from the chuck wagon.

"Grass grows back fast."

"I guess if you run cows over it only once a year or once every five years, they do no harm."

"Yeah," Chad said.

Jock steeled himself for his boss to have another spell, but Chad had eaten lightly that night and didn't seem to be in any discomfort.

"What is this ulcer thing you got, Chad?" Jock asked, as if to sound out Chad about another vomiting episode. "What is it, exactly?"

"Doc Ford says it's like a sore in my stomach."

"An open sore?"

"I don't know how open. Maybe like a boil, or maybe like a burn hole. He says the stomach acid when I eat, the stuff that digests food, makes it act up. He said I could cure it myself if I changed what I eat."

"Change what you eat?"

Chad laughed. His laugh was somewhat strained. "Yeah. Boiled chicken. Peaches. Oatmeal mush. Anything soft and tasteless, I reckon."

Jock thought about what Chad had said. "We ought to be able to corral some chickens along the way. Jubilee can boil 'em up for you. I don't know about the peaches. He might have some in an airtight."

"Nope. I'm not going to eat chicken when I raise beef. And there's not a peach this side of Georgia."

"Well, what does Doc Ford say about getting well if you don't eat chicken?"

"I'm not going to talk about that, Jock. Because I don't know and Doc Ford probably doesn't either."

"You're a stubborn bastard, Chad."

"The medicine helps. It might clear up once we get this herd to Ellsworth."

Jock shook his head and rolled a cigarette while Chad looked off into the sunset, a spectacular spray of shimmering golden light through gilt-edged clouds. Just above the horizon the sky looked like the banked fires of Vulcan himself, all deep red topped by soft salmon.

"Which reminds me, Jock. Been meaning to talk to you about something the whole time we've been out. Just never had the chance before."

"What's that?" Jock lit his cigarette, grateful that the wind had died away. He had burned his fingers more than once during the night, when he couldn't sleep and his craving for tobacco had a grip on him.

Chad waited until Jock had taken a couple of puffs on his cigarette.

"Rachael and Victoria are taking the stage to Ellsworth in a couple of months. I plan to meet them there," Chad said.

"That will be nice for them, and for you, Chad."

"You haven't seen Victoria in a couple of years, have you, Jock?"

"Little Vicky? No, I reckon not. Been about three years, maybe."

"She's not 'little Vicky' anymore. She's all grown up."

"I can't imagine."

"She always liked you. Talks about you all the time."

Jock was flattered, but he wondered where Chad was going with all this talk about Vicky.

"What is she now?" Jock asked. "About eighteen or so?"

"She's nineteen and she'll be twenty this year. In December."

"I remember. Right around Christmas. She was a cute little jigger."

"Cute as a speckled pup. But that was then. She's a raving beauty now. Looks like her mother. Only prettier."

"Well, Rachael's top drawer in the looks department," Jock said.

"I thought . . . you being alone now, and Twyla gone, you might be looking for a help-meet. Rachael thinks so, too. So does Victoria."

"A helpmeet?" Jock knew what Chad was driving at, but it was too soon. The memories of Twyla were still too strong, too vivid in his mind. Anyway, he had never thought of Vicky like that. In his mind, she was still a little freckle-faced girl with pigtails.

"You know. A wife. Someone to help you build up your ranch back to where it was, better than it was. You'll have money after this drive."

"Chad, I haven't even thought about remarrying. And maybe I never will."

A silence built up between them.

After a while, Chad stopped staring at the sunset. The sky in the west was all ashes now.

"Well, there it is, Jock. Something to ponder

over. Victoria will be right glad to see you again. She'd make you a fine wife."

"I'll ponder over it, Chad."

Chad started to walk away, back toward the campfire, when there was a ruckus off to the east. Men were lifting their voices and cattle bawled as a rider made his way to the fire.

"What the hell?" Chad said.

He walked around the wagon, and Jock followed him a moment later. He recognized the rider as Quist, who was weaving his way through the herd, leading a horse. There was something atop the other horse, slung across the saddle. At first Jock thought it was a calf, but as he walked up behind Chad, he heard what the men around the fire were saying.

"That's Burt's horse all right," Earl Foster said.

"Where's Burt?" a man named Ernesto Sandoval said. "I ain't seen him all day. He was supposed to be riding swing with me."

"There's a dead man on that there horse," Mac said.

"Sure as shootin'," Jubilee said. "Dead or conked out cold."

"Help Quist get through," Jock ordered, and some of the hands rose up and started moving cattle out of the way, swatting them on their rumps and twisting their tails.

Quist threaded his way through and rode

into camp, his features drawn, his eyes invisible in the dim light beyond the campfire.

"He's naked," Mac said, his voice stricken with shock.

Men rushed up to help pull the body off the horse. Jock walked over, along with Chad, as the men laid the dead man out on the ground, faceup.

"He was shot in the back," Quist said. "I found him after I saw two men ride off and the buzzards start to gather."

"Where's his shirt?" Chad asked.

Quist dismounted and shrugged. "Damned if I know. That's how I found Stubbins. Don't make no sense, if'n you ask me."

"Did you see if either of the men riding off had Burt's shirt with them?" Jock asked.

"Yeah, come to think of it, one of them was waving something."

"Recognize the men?" Jock asked.

Quist shook his head.

Burt Stubbins was stone cold. There was dried blood on his chest where the bullet had exited. It was plain that he had been shot in the back. The men all gathered around for a look. Some of them took their hats off out of respect.

Chad looked at Jock, a questioning look in his eyes. "Torgerson?" he asked.

"Maybe," Jock said. "Likely. And those two men Lou Quist saw might have been Fogarty and Clutter."

"Yeah. I forgot about those two. They were spotted just before that dust storm hit us."

Jock walked away from the body of Burt Stubbins. He spit out the remnants of his cigarette and rolled another one. He was thinking. Burt's death could not go unavenged. He was worried about the morale of the X8 hands at this latest development. If Clutter and Fogarty were ordered by Torgerson to kill X8 drovers, the hands might figure the drive wasn't worth it and just ride off back home.

Chad walked over as Jock was lighting his cigarette.

"What do you make of this, Jock?" he asked.

"I think," Jock said, "that Torgerson just declared war. And we have to track those bastards down and teach Curt a lesson."

"How are you going to do that?"

"Chad, I know how to fight a war. Just leave it to me."

Jock blew a plume of smoke into the air. The expression of dismay on Chad's face did not fade. It bloomed in the firelight like a death mask.

Chapter 21

Amos Beeson came back into camp late the next morning. The herd was already up and heading north.

"He looks like the wrath of God," Chad said to Jock.

Jock had been worried about Beeson, wondering if he had met the same fate as Burt Stubbins. So he was relieved to see Beeson, no matter that he looked like a man who had slept on a bed of cholla cactus all night.

"You're late, Amos," Jock said, half joking, his smile a wispy shadow under the smoke from his dangling cigarette. "Long ride?"

"Torgerson's behind us by at least a half day," Beeson said. His lips were cracked from dryness and the sun. "You got some water? I plumb run out."

Chad handed over his canteen to Beeson, who drank noisily for four or five seconds.

"God that tastes good."

"Anybody see you?" Jock asked as Beeson wiped his mouth with his sleeve.

He drank again and then handed the canteen back to Chad. "I don't reckon," Beeson said. "But I seen plenty. Heard more."

"What?" Jock asked.

"Saw Torgerson," Beeson said. "He was chasing after strays and found them in a creek that run through a little gully. I was up top when two fellers came riding up with a bloody shirt. One of them told Torgerson he got it off an X8 hand and they'd get him more. Torgerson said he'd pay them for each shirt they brung in. I like to froze plumb to death just shivering with the chilblains. I got the hell out of there."

Chad and Jock exchanged looks.

"It's like you figured, Jock."

"That bastard Torgerson has put a bounty on X8 hands," Jock said.

"He's lower than a skunk," Chad said.

"Why, what happened?" Beeson asked.

Jock told him about Burt Stubbins. Beeson's face drained of color when he heard about the shirtless body.

"Mr. Becker," Beeson said, "you're going to

lose every hand on this here drive if you don't put a stop to those two killers. I swear."

"Take it easy, Amos," Jock said. "I'll get those two, and Torgerson will hang for what he did to Burt."

"That's mighty damned comforting, Mr. Kane," Beeson said, a sarcastic twang to his already twangy voice. "Mighty damned comforting."

"I've already issued orders that no man on this drive is to ride alone, Amos," Jock said. "So, you find a partner and get back to work."

"What about the Apaches we saw?" Beeson asked. "You figured Torgerson made a deal with them, too. Looks like we got a whole passel of killers just waiting to pick us off. One by one."

"We can deal with the Apaches," Jock said. "Torgerson, too."

"I hope you're right," Beeson said.

"Get yourself some grub and pick out a partner, Amos," Jock said. "We've got a good lead on Torgerson now. I don't want to lose it."

Every rider for the X8 was on the alert from then on. The herd made its fifteen miles that day, and the next. Not only did the drovers keep each other in sight, they all had itchy

trigger fingers. They jumped at every jackrab-
bit, every roadrunner, every rattle of a side-
winder. Every drover's senses were honed to
a fine keenness, sharp as a Toledo blade.

Jock had spoken to Vic Cussler, right after
Beeson's return from his scouting job.

"You're going to have to be trail boss for a
few days, Vic," he said. "Think you can handle it?"

"I don't know, boss. I don't know this
country much. It's a lot of responsibility.
Why? You going someplace?"

"I might have to track those two killers
working for Torgerson. I need a good man to
mark the trail, find the water and the good
bedding ground. You've been watching me.
You should be able to handle the job."

"Well, I reckon I could. I can try anyways."

"That's all I ask. Just keep the herd heading
north and avoid trampling any ranches along
the way. You'll do fine."

"I appreciate your confidence in me, boss."

"You'll have Chad with you. He can help."

"That poor man is sick most of the time.
He won't be much help."

"He knows the country. But it's best if you
can rely on your own judgment, Vic."

"Right, boss."

Later that same day, when Jock and Vic had ridden back from finding a place to bed the herd for the night, two rifle shots sounded from somewhere to the east. Close, but not too close—loud enough to make Jock stiffen as he sat up straight in the saddle. The sound waves faded into a silence that echoed in Jock's brain long after they had wafted away from his ears. The herd lumbered on, un-phased by the whip-crack of the rifles.

Vic looked at Jock, his brows wrinkled in puzzlement.

"What do you make of it, Mr. Kane?"

"Let's find out," Jock said.

"Somebody shooting at jackrabbits, maybe."

"Those were two different rifles, Vic. The shots close together. Big caliber. Henrys, maybe."

The drovers watched the two as they galloped past the front of the herd and headed in the direction of the rifle reports. Jock noticed that some of the drovers had pulled their rifles from their scabbards. He waved to them, then gestured that they should stay put and tend to the herd.

Jock was not prepared for what he and Vic found. At first, they saw only two riderless horses standing next to each other, reins drooping like broken tethers. Both horses kept turning their heads, looking back at something neither he nor Vic could see.

"I know those horses," Vic said.

"So do I. They're from our remuda. Know who was riding them today?"

Vic shook his head.

A few moments later, the two men rode up to a grisly sight, some fifty or sixty yards from the riderless horses.

Jock swore under his breath.

Two men lay on the ground, one faceup, the other facedown. Both were naked to the waist, their shirts removed. Both had been shot in the back.

"Sonofabitch," Vic said aloud. "That's Gil Fuentes looking up at us."

"The other one is Manny, unless I'm mistaken."

Vic got down out of the saddle and turned Manny over.

"Yep, it's Manuel Rivera all right. Neither one of them had a chance, Mr. Kane."

"I wish you'd start calling me Jock, Vic. Now's as good a time as any."

"I feel like crying, Mr. . . . I mean, Jock. These were good boys. Hard workers. They knew cattle."

"I know," Jock said.

"I wonder why the killers took their shirts," Vic said.

"That's how they get their bounty for killing X8 hands."

"Huh?"

"Torgerson has put a bounty on every one of us. I think he looks at the bloody shirts with the holes in them for proof. Then he pays off the two men who murdered these two and any others."

"That no-good son of a bitch," Vic said in his slow, even drawl.

"Vic, I'm going to see to it that those two bastards never get to spend one cent of that blood money."

"How?" Vic asked.

"Let's get these two back up on their horses and take them back to the herd. That way, we can give them a proper burial tonight."

"You might have a mutiny on your hands, Mr. . . . ah, Jock. Once the boys see what happened to these two good, honest men, they'll all want to light a shuck for home."

"What about you, Vic?"

Vic didn't answer right away. He bunched up his lips and squeezed both eyes shut as if struggling with the question, as if he were weighing possible death against loyalty to the brand.

"I don't know, Jock. I just don't know. I ain't made my mind up."

"Fair enough. You think about it, because we're going to take these boys back to that big creek and I'm going to say words over them. Any man who wants to turn tail and run home to his mama can draw his pay."

"You'd let the hands go without a fight? Without an argument?"

"You can't buy loyalty, Vic. Either a man wants to ride for the brand, or he doesn't. I can't force men to do what they don't want to do."

Vic turned away. He tried not to look at the dead men, but Jock walked over and laid Fuentes out, straightening his crumpled body, putting his heels together and folding his arms across his chest. Then he did the same with the body of Manuel Rivera. He showed Vic a reverence that touched him. Vic shook his head, as if shaking off his bad feelings, and walked back to where the two dead men's horses were standing. Jock let him go to do it on his own. Let him have those few moments, just as the two dead men would have theirs, in a quiet state of repose, if only for a few minutes.

When Vic got back, they loaded Fuentes and Rivera on their horses and tied them on securely. The ignominy of this was not lost on either Jock or Vic, but there was no other way.

"Did you know these men well, Vic?" Jock asked as they were heading back to the herd.

"I knew Rivera better than Fuentes. He was a good, honest man. Fuentes, he was never no trouble. He did his work and he didn't grumble none about it."

That night, the dead men were laid out beside two holes dug six feet deep. Jock nodded to Horky and Pablo Cornejo, the two chosen to lay the corpses in their graves. Horky picked Rivera up by the shoulders, while Pablo lifted his feet. Both corpses were stiff by then. They laid him gently in his grave, then did the same with Fuentes. Then they took shovels and began to put the dirt back in the hole where Rivera lay, while Ernesto Sandoval and Ed Purvis shoveled dirt on Fuentes.

"Ashes to ashes and dust to dust," intoned Jock as the men stood next to the graves, their hats in their hands. "Almighty God," he said, "please let these boys into heaven and give them good horses to ride, some gold in their pockets and a soft bed to sleep in at night. We give these good men into your kind and merciful hands. Amen."

Many of the men muttered, "Amen," as well.

Quist, however, glared at Jock Kane with eyes so malevolent they might have been forged in hell on the devil's own anvil.

"Jock," Quist said, "I'm calling you out, you sonofabitch. You good as killed those men yourself, and I aim to see you join them in the ground."

Jock looked away from the grave and straight into Quist's eyes. The shoveling ceased and there was not a sound, not even a breath, among the men there.

It might have been the longest moment in a man's life, just then, with death hovering over them just as surely as two men lay dead in the ground.

Chapter 22

Jock fixed Quist with eyes that seemed to smoke like the fuse on a stick of dynamite. Jock turned slightly to square himself with the man who had accused him of murder. He did not assume a fighting stance, but showed Quist that he was ready if Quist wanted to open the ball and dance.

"We just buried two men, Quist," Jock said. "Do you want to make it a threesome?"

"I just don't like what you done, Kane."

"What did I do?"

"You had us all double up. You said it would be safer that way. Now, we got two men killed, 'stead of one. Seems to me you don't know what the hell you're doing."

"You've got a point, Quist. I thought it

would be safer if we watched out for each other. I was wrong."

"Dead wrong," Quist said.

"Now, hold on," Chad said. "Let's not fight amongst each other over this. Lou, you back off. Jock, let's let our tempers cool."

Young Mac's eyes were like a pair of boiled eggs, bulging from their sockets. His mouth hung long and slack as if he were witnessing a pair of Roman gladiators from the arena itself. Jubilee stood next to his helper, the lower hem of his food-stained apron wadded up in his hands, the cloth soaking up his sweat. Dub Morley licked his dry lips, his eyes flickering with the firelight, like the eyes of a hungry cat. Horky's eyes were still wet from weeping over his dead brethren. He crossed himself. His lips moved in a silent prayer to the Virgin Mary.

"Lou's right, though, Mr. Becker. Kane's done put us all in danger with his fool orders."

Chad looked at Morley, the man who had spoken.

"He did what he thought was right," Chad said. "I agreed with him."

"And look what it got us," Morley said. "Two more dead men."

"You stay out of this, Dub," Quist said.

Morley's eyes glittered like polished agates.

The sun sank like a stone in black water and the night sky sprouted stars. Flame shadows licked the faces of the men standing around the fire, giving their heads the look of hideous masks. They smelled blood, Jock knew, and one wrong move could see the air filled with flying lead. Quist was the man he had to back down, but the others were ready to take sides in a fight. He and Chad would be caught in the middle, like bugs in a spider's web.

"This is not the way, Quist," Jock said. "Would you do Torgerson's work for him? He wants to kill us all so he can get to Ellsworth before we do. Think about it."

"The way I see it, Kane, you're the burr under our saddle. We can handle those two killers our way. Not yours." Quist stood his ground, defiant, his arms bowed out away from his body, one hand hovering close to the six-gun in his holster.

"Kane, your word don't mean shit around here," Quist said. "Three men are dead already. You've been a jinx on this drive, same as you was when you drove your own herd up to Kansas. Only you never made it. I'm getting the same feeling about this one."

"I have a plan," Jock said. "It'll take some

doing. I'll need every man jack of you to pull it off. But we'll get those boys."

"What's your plan?" Dub Morley asked.

"We'll put it together in the morning," Jock said. "Now, get to your herd or get some sleep if you're not riding nighthawk. Quist?"

Jock threw out the challenge and every head turned toward Quist.

He shuffled his feet, staring down at the toes of his boots as he worried some dirt.

"I reckon I can wait one more day," Quist said. "But this plan better work, Kane. I ain't going to cut you much slack."

"Fair enough," Jock said, and turned away. The others sighed and walked to the fire or to their horses. The men with the shovels finished mounding up the dirt over the two graves.

Chad drew Jock aside.

"This plan of yours, Jocko. Is it going to work?"

"I hope like hell it does, Chad."

The next day, Jock found the place he was looking for, having ridden off alone, leaving Cussler to find a noon stop for the chuck wagon. The place he chose was a spring-fed pond surrounded by trees. There was enough deadwood around to make a fire, and enough green wood to make smoke if he cut it from the water oaks. Satisfied, he rode back and started speaking to certain drovers he encountered, pulling them away from the herd without explanation. But he did not pick the men at random. He had thought about who he wanted to take back to the pond and his choices were deliberate.

They gathered around the chuck wagon—Jock, Lou Quist, Dub Morley, Fred Naylor, Earl Foster, Julio Horcasitas and Ernesto Sandoval.

"Don't you want me to go with you, Jocko?" Chad asked.

"Yes, I want you there, Chad. Now, here's what we need to take with us." Jock listed the items: two shirts, two pair of trousers, the two hats once worn by Fuentes and Rivera when they were alive, some empty flour sacks, a shovel, hatchets, a hammer, nails, a saw and, finally, two horses from the remuda. He did not explain why he wanted these items, but Jubilee supplied the flour sacks and tools.

"Follow me," Jock said, and the strange caravan set out while Mac and Jubilee watched them go, both scratching their heads.

"He's got something up his sleeve," Jubilee said to Mac.

"Yeah," Mac said. "I sure wish I knew

where they were going and what they're going to do."

"We'll find out in due time, Mac."

At the water hole, Jock put the men to work.

"Dub, you dig two holes where I show you," Jock said. "Big enough to sink some sticks in them." He marked out the places for the holes. He had others gather firewood, both dry and green, and stack it near the two holes Dub was digging. Then he had Horky cut some straight limbs from mesquite trees, and cut the trunks of the smaller ones. He and Chad filled the flour sacks with dirt and tied them at the openings, leaving a loop in each knot.

"What the hell is all this for?" Quist asked.

"We're going to set a trap for those two killers," Jock said.

"It don't make no sense," Quist grumbled.

"It will," Jock said. "Horky, stack that firewood high, deadwood at the bottom, green leaves and limbs on top."

When Dub finished digging the holes to Jock's satisfaction, he and Chad nailed the straight limbs into crosses. They set the long ends into the holes, filled them with dirt and tamped them down. Then Jock put the sacks of dirt atop the crosses. He put shirts on the cross bars of the Ts, and set hats over the sacks. Then he laid out the pants and he and Chad filled them with dirt so that they looked like legs.

"Now all of you walk off a ways, look at those dummies, then come back."

Reluctantly, Quist and the others walked several yards away. Jock waved them to walk still farther away. When they were two hundred yards off, he waved them back toward the water hole.

"Now," Jock said, "tell me what you saw, Quist. What did those dummies look like?"

Quist looked puzzled.

"I reckon it looked like two men sitting down."

"Yeah," Morley said. "Sort of."

"From a distance, if you saw those dummies sitting by a fire, you'd think they were a couple of drovers cooking a meal, wouldn't you?" Jock said.

The men all nodded.

"Those dummies won't really fool anyone, Kane," Quist said.

"We'll see," Jock said. "Horky, I want you to saw through the long part of the crosses. Not enough so that the limbs break, but

221

enough so that they'll break easy if, say, a bullet hits anyplace on the wood. Can you do that?"

Horky nodded. He got the saw, knelt down and began to saw at the bottom of a limb that served as the longest part of the cross.

Jock looked over the scene himself, walking around, checking the stack of wood. The men watched him as if observing some arcane ritual that made no sense to them.

"Now," Jock said, "we light the fire, hide out, and wait."

"For what?" Quist asked.

"Maybe for a couple of rifle shots," Jock said. He pointed to the southeast. "They'll be coming in from that direction, I reckon. They'll see the smoke from the fire and want to investigate. Then they'll ride up and see those two hobbled horses, two men sitting by the fire and figure it's an easy way to make money."

"What if they come from another direction?" Chad asked.

"We'll be north of this, out of sight, but ready to ride. If they shoot and think they've killed the two dummies, they'll want to retrieve the shirts for proof of their kill. We'll ride up, surround them and . . ."

Jock touched the coiled lariat on his saddle

as his voice trailed off. Nobody asked the next question.

When Horky was finished with the sawing, Jock ordered them all to head north and ride until they could no longer see the fictitious campsite, nor be seen by anyone beyond that point.

"I'll light the fire and join you shortly," Jock said.

When all the men were out of sight, Jock rolled a cigarette. He lit it and then touched the match to the shavings he had put at the bottom of the pyramid of wood. The shavings caught and soon the fire was blazing. As it licked at the leaves and green branches, smoke began to spiral upward. Satisfied, Jock mounted his horse and rode away. He hoped they would not have to wait long for his trap to work.

The men sat their horses and looked at the smoke rising in the sky. There was no breeze, no wind, and the sky was blue and cloudless. They fingered their rifles, and once in a while Quist looked at Kane, with that cigarette dangling from his mouth, a picture of calmness while everyone's nerves were jangling like a brass wind chime. Nobody spoke. Everyone listened.

Jock did not look at any of them, nor did

he look at the column of smoke in the sky. Instead, he stared at his horse's ears, which were like two sharp cones rising from its head. The horse would hear approaching riders long before he or any of the men would. And then he would know whether or not his plan was going to work. The only sounds were the switching of the horses' tails and the soft drone of flies avoiding the swatting brooms.

Chad looked at Jock. He opened his mouth to speak, but Jock put a finger to his lips, then cupped his ear.

Chad nodded.

A few moments later, Jock's horse whickered low in its throat. Its ears stiffened, then twisted one way, then another.

Jock sat up straight. He eased his rifle from its scabbard, then looked at the others. They all pulled their rifles from their sheaths and laid them across their pommels. Hours seemed to pass in the space of a few seconds.

There was the whip-crack of a rifle. Then, another. Then, a split second of utter stillness in an eternity of silence.

Chapter 23

D.F. was the first to spot the smoke. He reached over and punched Clutter on the arm.

"Looky there, Randy."

"Yeah, D.F., smoke. A long ways off, though."

"What you reckon it is?"

"Maybe Becker's got him a running iron. Curt said this morning he was missing some cattle."

"Boy, I'd like to catch them boys rustling Cross J cattle."

"About all you're likely to catch is a dose of the clap, D.F."

"Oh, come on, Randy, don't make fun of me."

"It's hard not to, D.F."

They rode toward the smoke. It was only a

thin tendril in the distance and it would take them a good half hour to reach it on horseback. D.F. was excited, but Randy was worrying his lower lip, sliding inside his mouth and wadding his tongue up against it as if it were a wad of tobacco.

"What was you and Abel talking about last night, Randy?" D.F. crowded his horse in close to Clutter's.

"Nothing much."

"Yeah? You was talking a real long time."

"Abel found out we was on the bounty. I reckon Curt must have told him."

"So, did he want in on it?"

"Naw, he just asked me not to shoot his brother Jock in the back."

"I thought he and Jock were on the outs."

"They are, I reckon."

"So, why'd he ask us not to put Jock down?"

"He said he wanted to do it hisself."

"Haw," D.F. cackled, slapping his leg in glee. "You know why, Randy?"

"Yeah, I know why."

"Why?"

"Cause Abel is scared shitless of Jock."

"That's right. Abel says Jock will kill him on sight because of what Abel done to that pretty little wife of Jock's."

They drew closer to the smoke.

"Curt wants it that way," Randy said.

"What way?"

"Torgerson figures he might have a run-in with Jock Kane and he wants to sic Abel on him."

"Whooee. I'd pay money to see that," D.F. squealed.

"You'd pay money to see two dogs get hooked up, D.F."

"No, I'd throw water on 'em, Randy." D.F. thought that was a funny answer and he laughed at himself.

Randy was silent, looking at the smoke. They were close enough now, and could smell it. Randy spotted the fire by the water hole and reined up. D.F. put his horse beside Randy's and looked, too.

"Damn," D.F. said, "there's two of 'em right there, and they got their backs to us."

"Yeah. I wonder what they're doing way out here. I don't see no cattle." Randy pulled his rifle out of its scabbard.

"Hell, they're probably hunting strays and got hungry or something. Or—maybe they ain't X8 hands. What then, Randy?"

"Hell, they got shirts on, don't they?" Randy said.

D.F. hefted his rifle, then cocked it. "Let's put 'em down," he said.

"You take the one on the right, D.F. I'll take the other'n."

Both men readied their rifles, then brought them to their shoulders. They took aim. Randy fired first. Then, a split second later, D.F. shot. They watched both figures move, one falling over on its side, the other face-first.

"Got 'em," D.F. said.

"They sure fell funny," Randy said, squinting his eyes.

"Hell, they fell, didn't they? Let's go get their shirts. Boy, I can feel fresh money burning a hole in my pocket."

The two men rode up to the water hole at a gallop. Both had their rifles at the ready in case one or the other of the shot men were still alive.

As Randy reined up, he saw movement off to one side. D.F. saw something on his right.

In moments, the two men knew they had made a mistake.

"We done stepped into shit," D.F. said.

"Just drop those rifles, boys," Jock said. "We all got a bead on you both. One twitch and you're dead men."

"Don't shoot," D.F. said, dropping his rifle.

"Well, damned if it ain't Jock Kane," Randy said. Then he let his rifle fall to the ground.

He looked at the two dummies, then back at Jock.

"D.F.," Randy said, "looky there, would you? We done shot two scarecrows."

D.F. looked at the piles of limp clothing and his eyes widened.

"We been hoodwinked, Randy," D.F. said.

The men of the X8 rode up and removed the pistols from Randy and D.F.'s holsters.

"Keep your hands in the air," Jock said.

"What you aiming to do, Kane?" Randy asked.

"You boys will hang from that water oak yonder," Jock said.

"For what? Shooting a couple of damned scarecrows?" Randy sounded indignant.

"Yeah, we ain't done nothing," D.F. said.

"Horky, tie their hands behind their backs," Jock ordered. "Quist, you help him."

"You can't do this, Kane. We're innocent men. You ain't got no cause."

"Clutter, you've killed three of my men, you and Fogarty. Now you're going to hang."

"Prove it," Randy said.

"I don't have to, Clutter. I caught you trespassing on X8 land. Trying to steal two horses. And I'm the law here." Jock pulled out the makings of a cigarette as he stared at the two outlaws.

"This ain't nobody's land," Randy said. "And we weren't stealing no horses."

"Witnesses saw you both shoot my men dead. Say your prayers, boys. Chad, shake out a couple of ropes."

Randy's face drained of color. D.F., his hands tied behind his back, leaned over and vomited. Some of it spilled down his shirt. Horky made his horse sidle away from the mess and the smell.

Chad shook out his lariat and Fred Naylor strung his rope out, and began making a hangman's loop. Quist finished tying Randy's hands behind his back with leather thongs.

"Take them over under that oak tree," Jock ordered.

Quist nodded. He and Horky led the outlaws' horses over to the tree and placed them beneath a strong limb. They held onto the reins while Chad and Fred finished making hangman's loops. The other men rode over and surrounded the two killers, looking at them with dull, glazed eyes.

"Earl, get some water and put out that fire," Jock said.

Randy sat up straight in the saddle and looked at the men standing around in a half circle. His gaze went to each one, then stopped when he fixed a look on Dub Morley.

Dub stiffened and shifted his gaze, as if trying to avoid being noticed.

"Dub," Randy said, "you ought to be up here right alongside us."

Everyone there looked at Dub. The man said nothing.

Jock lit his cigarette, letting it dangle from his lips. He smiled a thin smile.

That statement from Randy only served to confirm Jock's suspicions about Dub Morley. But he had to find out for sure.

"What did you mean by that, Clutter?" Jock asked.

"Dub's on Torgerson's pay sheet, same as us. Fact is, he's the one told us where the easiest targets was when we first set out."

"That's right," D.F. said. "Go ahead, Kane, ask old Dub there. He's been a spy for Torgerson ever since you set out. Ain't that right, Dub?"

Dub squirmed as Jock skewered him with a look.

"Well, what about it, Dub?" Jock asked. "Any truth to what these boys are saying?"

"They're lying through their teeth," Dub said. But his face was blanched like the skin of a boiled pullet and sweat streaks drooled from his sideburns like liquid worms.

"That so?" Jock said. "Well, I've been watching you, Dub, and I've had my suspicions."

"About what?" Dub seemed ready to tough it out. Randy and D.F. looked down on the man with contempt as Dub squirmed like a rabbit caught in a snare.

"Like you killing that Cross J hand, for one thing. And not being where you ought to be or being someplace you shouldn't be."

"I thought that man was an Apache," Dub said. "Or with 'em."

"No, you killed him because he knew you. You didn't want him to spill the beans. Isn't that right?"

"No, it ain't."

Jock looked at the others gathered around. "Any of you think Dub here is a murderer, same as these two we caught red-handed? We can hang three as easy as two."

"This is a damned kangaroo court," Dub said. "I ain't done nothing, Kane. Your suspicions be damned."

Jock waited as those around him pondered Dub's fate, but none of them said anything.

"Quist, what about you?" Jock asked. "You wanted an end to the killings. But Dub here is a spy for Torgerson. Should we hang him or just give him a good whipping and send him back to Torgerson?"

"I don't know if Dub is guilty or not. I can't just kill a man."

"You've been mighty ready to kill me, Quist," Jock said, a hard edge to his voice.

"That's different. I got a grudge against you, Kane."

"Well, I've got a grudge against these men. All three of them, Dub included. Do you ride for the brand, or don't you?"

Quist thought it over. "I reckon I ride for Mr. Becker."

"And so do we. But not Dub or these other two."

"I say we hang Dub, too," Chad said. "I think he killed that Cross J hand in cold blood. And if he told these boys where to find my men and shoot them, he's just as guilty as they are."

There was a low murmur of assent from the other men.

Dub started to run, but Horky caught him by the arm, spun him around and threw a fist into his face. He fell to his knees, dazed.

Jock reached for the rope on his saddle and shook it out. He handed it to Horky.

"Put a loop in that, Horky, and Fred, you strip Dub of his pistol and tie his hands behind him.

Dub started sniveling as Fred jerked him to his feet and tied his hands behind him. Fred and Horky lifted Dub into his saddle and led his horse over to Clutter and Fogarty.

Jock spit out his cigarette and mounted his horse. He took one of the ropes, slid it over Fogarty's head and tightened it around his neck. Then he slung the bitter end over the tree limb. He did the same with Clutter and Morley. Chad took the rope ends and wrapped them around the tree trunk behind the three men. He knotted them all together.

"May you burn in hell, Kane," Dub said, and then began to cry. His body shook with the paroxysms.

Jock rode up behind the three horses and raised his arm. He slapped the rump of each one. The horses bolted out from under their riders and the three men swung from the tree, kicking as they struggled for their last breaths.

Horky crossed himself.

Jock dug in his pocket for the makings.

"When they're dead, get them down," Jock said. "Then tie their bodies to their horses and take them back to where Torgerson is. Maybe he'll get the idea."

Quist looked at Jock with something close to admiration.

"Kane," he said, "you're a hard man—you know that?"

"I'm as hard as I have to be," Jock said, and rolled a quirly in the sudden stillness of the afternoon.

Chapter 24

At first, Rufus Cobb thought he was seeing a mirage. And he was, but there was more to it than a dancing mirror, a shimmering lake conjured up by the blazing sun as it scoured the plain on its long arc toward the west. For out of the phantom waters that flowed like quicksilver over the earth some two hundred yards away, he saw three horses emerge, plodding toward him like exhausted beasts of burden, humps on their backs, their silhouettes strange and misshapen as if they were not horses at all, but odd beasts as illusory as the scintillating silver waters that rose and fell around their legs.

He rode toward them, wary, disbelieving, and saw the lake vanish like the mirage it was. He rubbed his eyes with a balled-up fist, but the horses, or what appeared to be horses, remained, stepping slowly toward him, their heads bowed low, part of their cargo dripping below their bellies, below the stirrups of their saddles. Rufus blinked and squeezed his eyes tight, then opened them quickly as if expecting the strange horses to disappear, to be gone, like the waters that never were.

Cobb smelled death as he rode up to the lead horse. Now he knew that those were bodies tied to the horses and as he grabbed the reins of the first horse, his stomach churned and he felt bile rise up in his throat. The other horses stopped and he forced himself to look at those, too, as well as their grisly cargo.

He recognized the horses now, but he did not recognize the men, although he knew who they were. Their faces were turned from him, facing the ground. He saw the ropes around their necks, and the stench added to his feeling of suffocation. He felt a tightness around his own neck as if it, too, were ringed by a rope, shutting off the oxygen.

"Good Lord," he said softly and his stomach bucked inside him, boiled with acids so that he had to turn away and fight down the vomit that threatened to rise up into his throat and mouth.

He looked around, wanting to call to someone, but there were no drovers near him, and he knew he was alone.

"Suffering Jesus," he muttered. He had to think hard to remember where Torgerson might be at that late hour of the day. The horses threw long shadows on the ground as he gathered up the other reins in his hand so that he had all three animals under his control. The cattle stared at him from a distance and their ears stiffened. Some of them began to moan deep in their throats and he wondered if they were going to run as he passed them, riding toward the head of the herd where he knew Torgerson and others would be. He could not look at the dead men anymore. He had seen their faces starting to swell and bloat, the ropes so tight around their throats that their heads resembled hideous balloons. Their bowels had emptied and filled their pants, staining them as the fecal matter soaked through.

Cobb saw Ed Timmons and knew he was near the head of the herd. Ed, curious perhaps, rode out to meet him.

"What you got there, Rufus?" Ed said.

"Where's Torgerson?" Rufus said.

"He's up yonder with Rafe." Ed's nose crinkled up as he smelled the scent of death.

He swore under his breath. "Curt ain't going to like this none," he said. "That's Clutter, ain't it?"

"And D.F. and Dub," Rufus said.

"What are them ropes doing around their necks?"

"What the hell do you think, Ed? These boys have been hanged."

"Sonofabitch," Timmons said.

Torgerson saw them coming and called out to Rafe Castle. Castle rode toward Torgerson, but his eyes were on Cobb and the three horses he was leading.

"What happened, Rufus?" Torgerson said. "Who are those men?"

Cobb told him. Castle pinched his nose with his fingers as he rode up.

"Them horses just come up on me like you see 'em, Mr. Torgerson," Cobb said. "Liked to make me puke."

Torgerson rode up to each of the dead men as if to make sure that they were dead. He scowled when he saw the body of Dub Morley. His shoulders slumped in defeat and a terrible rage began to build. It was as if someone had exploded a bomb inside him. He sat up straight in the saddle and his body seemed to swell and expand.

"Jock Kane did this," he said. "Jock Kane

murdered these three men in cold blood. He had no right to hang them. Especially Dub."

"Yes, sir," Rafe said. "Jock sure did wrong here."

"Where's that bastard brother of his? Where's Abel Kane?" Torgerson roared like a madman and the men shrunk away as if they had been seared by the fire from a blast furnace.

"He's riding swing today," Rafe said. "Over yonder, the other side of the herd."

"Somebody go get him. I want him to see this. And then I want these men buried proper. Hear me?" Torgerson's eyes blazed with a hellish fire.

"I'll run get him," Rafe said. "I know just where he is."

Torgerson jerked his reins viciously and turned his horse away from the dead men. He rode a short distance, then made the horse pace back and forth over the same ground, like a man walking a jail cell. He clenched his fists as if he wanted to squeeze the life out of someone and his breathing made sounds through his nose that were not unlike a bull snorting.

The horses carrying the dead men stood hipshot, their heads drooping as if they had come back from a battle that they had lost.

Cobb wanted to be anywhere but where he was, and he turned his head one way, then another, trying to avoid the disgusting smell of death and offal that arose from the corpses.

Finally, Rafe returned, with Abel Kane following close behind.

"Did you tell him anything, Rafe?" Torgerson asked.

Rafe shook his head. "Just said you wanted to see him right away."

"What's . . . ?" Abel started to speak, then saw the dead men draped over their saddles. His mouth stayed open, but no sound came out.

"Take a look, Abel," Torgerson said. "Take a good look. Those are your pards yonder."

Abel hesitated. Rafe prodded him in the back with a stiffened finger. Abel rode over and looked at the dead men, turning his head slightly as if he could avoid the smell of them. He gagged and held on to his saddle horn until he could take a deep enough breath to keep his food down.

"Recognize them, Abel?" Torgerson said in a mocking tone. "They were all alive this morning. Laughing, joking, talking, smoking cigarettes, eating grub."

Abel turned away from the dead men and rode over to Torgerson.

"Who in hell did this, Mr. Torgerson? Those were good boys. Good friends."

"You want to know who hanged those boys? Without a trial or anything. Just strung 'em up to a tree and made them dance until the breath was all choked out of them. You want to know? Do you?"

"Yes, damn it. I want to know," Abel said.

"Your brother, Abel. Jock did this to them. He put ropes around their necks and hanged them and then sent them back here for you to see. For all of us to see what he did."

"That bastard," Abel said.

Torgerson let what had happened sink in. He watched Abel digest the full brunt of what he had seen and what he had been told. He wanted him to take it all in and let it turn his heart to the hardest stone.

Abel drew a finger across his face under one eye. Tears were starting to spill from the lids. He gulped in air and drew himself up straight in the saddle. But his eyes were wet and his lips quivered as a quiet rage slowly began to build inside him.

"You rode with those two boys, Randy and D.F.," Torgerson said. "You rode with them and you ate with them and you slept next to them at night. Well, they ain't no more. Not now. Your brother Jock hanged them in the bloom of their youth."

"Why?" Abel asked. "They never did anything to him."

"Jock's a madman," Torgerson said, knowing he didn't need any hard evidence for such a claim. The dead bodies spoke loudly enough in defense of that theory. "He's gone plumb crazy, Abel. Didn't you tell me he almost killed you? Tried to kill you?"

"Well, yeah, but he had good reason."

"Your brother's lost all reason now. Just look at those poor men, cut down in the prime of their lives."

Abel looked back at the dead men, then quickly returned his focus to Torgerson.

"What are you going to do about it, Mr. Torgerson?"

"I'm not going to do anything about it, Abel. But you are."

"Me?"

"Yeah, you. You're going after your brother and take him down."

"You mean kill him?"

"He tried to kill you."

"I know, but . . ."

"If you don't want to do it, just say so, son.

I'll get someone else to do the job. But somebody's got to see that these poor dead men did not die and have their killer go unpunished. Somebody has to avenge their deaths."

Abel thought for a long moment as the silence rose up around him like a huge ocean wave. The cattle rumbled by them, giving up their scents of gas and manure and musty hides, their breaths reeking of chewed and digested grasses and mesquite berries. The aroma mingled with that of the dead men and added weight to the silence, weight and much meaning.

"I could kill him," Abel said, finally. "I reckon I could. He blamed me for something I didn't do and I think he aims to kill me someday."

"That's what he said, didn't he?"

"Yeah, Mr. Torgerson. He said he was going to kill me if he ever saw me again."

"But he won't be expecting you to come after him, Abel. You can get the jump on Jock. You can kill him easier than he killed those men over there. One shot. One good shot. Right to the heart. And then it's over. All of it. You'll be free to live your life. You got a good ranch to go back to and you can marry and raise kids and cattle just like ordinary folks."

"Yeah, I could," Abel said in a day-dreaming tone of voice.

"Then go ahead and do it, Abel. And I'll see to it that you're rewarded for your efforts. I can't spare anyone to help you, so you'll have to go after Jock on your own. You can do that, can't you? You're a grown man and you're not afraid of your brother."

"No, I guess not. I'm not afraid of Jock. I just wish he had never been born, damn him."

Torgerson smiled and patted Abel on the shoulder.

"Come back when you've done the job," Torgerson said, and turned his horse away. He issued orders for the dead men to be buried.

Abel rode off alone, to the west. He rode as if he were in a daze, but he was thinking hard.

Jock had not been much of a brother to him. He was older and he had gone to the war. Then he married Twyla and their folks had died. Abel had grown up pretty much alone, not knowing his brother all that well. Torgerson was right. Jock meant to kill him one day. Well, Jock had another thing coming. "That ranch is partly mine," he said to himself, "but you'd never know it. Jock never gave me anything but a hard time."

Abel talked himself into killing his brother. But as he rode, he couldn't help thinking of that bible verse. It kept thrumming in his head like a worrisome part of a song. He heard it long after he rode into the dark skies of evening and could hear the X8 cattle lowing in the distance as they bedded down for the night.

"And Cain slew Abel."

Chapter 25

The Apaches picked a good place to start cutting cows out of the X8 herd. Jock had split the herd to make it easier to circumnavigate a ranch that was in the way and avoid mixing his cattle with those grazing there, and vice versa. The X8 cattle had been making progress with good weather, averaging fifteen miles a day. Quite a feat for a herd of that size, everyone said.

The attack didn't amount to a hill of beans, as the drovers said later. This was because Jock had planned well, and his scouts were ready for the raid. Horky was the man who picked up the tracks and figured out what the Apaches planned to do, and so Quist, Beeson, and the others were all banded together to thwart any rustling by the Apaches.

Jock had changed his strategy for the drive while they encircled the ranch in question, Mort Lamont's Lazy L. The cattle were in the lead and were strung out for several miles, streaming in a long, thin line. This made it more difficult for the drovers since they could not ride swing on such a lengthy bunch, but the cattle moved faster because they weren't stumbling into one another as they proceeded northward.

Horky showed Quist the Apache tracks, easy to spot, because the warriors all rode unshod ponies. He also showed him and the others the line the Apaches were taking, which led to a long draw just east of the herd.

"They will wait until the herd is almost passed," Horky said, "and then come out of that draw, cut so many head out and run them back into the draw and out the other end. They will pick a part of the herd where there is no swing rider and the men riding drag are too far away to see anything."

"How do you know all this, Horky?" Quist asked.

Horky smiled. "I am part Apache, and my grandfather told me many stories."

"I thought you were a Mexican."

"That is what I am. And a Mexican is part Spanish and part Indian. I am part Apache."

"Be damned," Quist said.

Horky smiled again.

"So, how do we stop them?" Quist asked. "How do we win a fight with them?"

"We can become Apaches for a little while," Horky said.

"Huh? How do we do that?"

"They will leave their horses down in the draw and walk up to the herd," Horky said. "They will pick out the cattle they want and herd them back down into the draw. Others will wait at the edge to guard those that steal and they will have no horses with them either. We must leave our horses, cover ourselves with dirt and grass, and crawl toward the place where the Apaches come out to steal the cattle."

"That don't sound like something a white man can do, Horky."

"We can do it," Beeson said. "I've seen Apaches rise up out of the ground where they've been lying for hours. You can't tell them from the grass."

"He is right," Horky said.

"I don't like it none, but if that's the only way, let's get to it."

And so they did. Nine men hobbled their horses well out of sight of the draw. Then they walked back within view of it, sat down and began smearing their faces and hands with dirt. Horky showed them how to pull grass and put it in their hat bands and in back of their necks. Then they lay on their bellies, rifles cocked, and started to crawl, following Horky. It was slow going but, finally, Horky stopped. He turned and motioned for the men to spread out and then lie still. It was then that the other scouts could hear the faint sounds of men down in the draw. Men and ponies, walking around, shuffling. They could smell the smoke from their pipes. They all heard some sounds they could not identify.

"What's that noise down there?" Beeson asked.

"They're whittling," Horky said.

"Whittling?"

"Sharpening sticks. They make the cattle prods to use to make the cows move."

As the herd passed by, close to the draw, Apaches began to emerge, slithering over the edge like lizards. The Indians looked all around and the scouts remained very still as Horky had told them they must do.

Each of the braves carried freshly sharpened sticks and they slid through the grass like stalking cats, making no sound. The Indians were barely visible, but the scouts could track them by their movements. Then, as if on some silent signal, the Apaches stood up well inside the body of the herd.

They prodded cows and moved them against the stream and out into the open. The cattle began bawling and lowing.

"When?" Quist whispered to Horky.

"Now," Horky said.

The scouts all got to their feet, but remained crouched.

"Charge them," Quist ordered, taking command. "Shoot them down, then hightail it for the draw and kill those Apaches down there."

Horky wanted to move closer before attacking, but the decision was taken out of his hands. On the heels of Quist's order, the scouts rose up as one man and started running toward the marauding Apaches. They fired their rifles on the run and, following Horky's lead, they zigzagged, staying hunched over. The Apaches tried to scatter, but the expert riflemen brought them down. The stolen cattle reversed course and ran back into the herd. The herd flared away from the gunfire and began to stampede. At first, only a few cattle were running full tilt, but then the contagion caught and soon the entire eastern wall of the herd was in full flight, adding to the confusion.

Quist and the others ran to the edge of the

draw and began picking out targets. The Apaches were mounting up and many were shot before they could jump on their ponies' backs. Others returned fire and got mounted. These were shot down like the proverbial fish in a barrel. The scouts were shouting to each other.

"Got one," Beeson said.

"Me, too," another man yelled.

The bloodlust was hot in their veins as the scouts slaughtered the hapless Apaches caught in the open at the bottom of the draw. Not a single one escaped, much to Quist's satisfaction.

"Lou, we done started a stampede," Beeson said, turning around from the rim of the draw.

"Damn," Quist said. "We've got to turn that herd."

He sounded disappointed and Horky looked at him.

"Well," Quist said, "I was thinking of taking me a few scalps to show Mr. Becker and Kane."

Horky turned away in disgust and began trotting back to retrieve his horse. Dead Apaches lay sprawled in the dirt, their blood soaking into the earth. Horky was sick to his stomach and he had to fight against stopping to heave up his guts.

The horses were in a blind panic when Horky, Quist, Beeson and the others ran up to retrieve them. Their high-pitched whinnies were cries of alarm that spread to the cattle, causing more of the herd to join the wild stampede. Horky fought with the hobbles and then had to hold onto the reins with tremendous effort to keep his horse from bolting. The others had much the same problem, and the men yelled and fought to bring their horses under control so that they could climb back up into their saddles.

Dust arose from the thundering herd as it surged northward, and by the time Horky did mount his horse, he could barely see the other men. He heard Quist cursing at his horse, then saw him put his boot in the left stirrup and haul himself up into the saddle. He rode over to him.

"It will be hard to turn this herd from where we are, Lou. Do you not agree?"

"Yeah, damned hard. You're on your own, Horky. I'm going to ride ahead and see if there's anything I can do. I have to outrun the herd if I can."

"I will go with you."

"Suit yourself. This is going to be hard as hell on the horses."

Jock was way ahead of the herd when he heard the thunder. The sound almost stopped his heart, for he knew what it was. The cattle had been docile for days, inured to the trail as if it were a normal pursuit for bovine creatures. They were stopped at eleven every morning while the cowhands came to the chuck wagon for noon grub. In the afternoons they ate up miles at a good pace, knowing there would be water and rest at the end of the day. At night, they'd rise up around midnight and then lie back down again, and might do that every hour. But they would stay put because the nighthawks gave them comfort with their low, throaty voices and their pleasant, soothing songs.

But now Jock knew he had a wild herd on his hands. He glanced over at Ringler, whose horse was also halted, its ears stiff and turning in every direction, its muscles quivering under its sleek hide.

"Jock," Ringler said, without finishing his sentence.

"We've got to turn that herd," Jock said. "We'll start with Calico Sal."

Both men turned their horses south and rode toward the sound of the rumbling. Before they even reached the herd, they could see the cloud of dust beginning to form like a gauzy brown-orange cloud. Jock knew then that the stampede didn't just involve a few hundred head, but perhaps the entire herd. At least, he thought, most of them were running in the right direction.

There was no sign of Calico Sal. By then, Jock knew, she was no longer the single leader. All of the cattle in the front of the herd served in that capacity. In fact, most of them had held their positions for all of the drive. But Sal and the other leaders had been swallowed up by the rampaging cattle behind them and were just more sets of horns slicing through the air.

Jock swore. Cattle were running everywhere, off to the left and to the right, and gaining momentum as if their rumps were on fire and the devil himself was chasing them with a pitchfork.

Jock and Dewey took off their hats and waded into the leaders nearest them, waving their Stetsons and yelling at the top of their voices.

"Whoa up."

"Hey, hey," they yelled, trying to turn the leaders and start the front part of the herd to milling.

The cattle ignored them and broke course to stream on either side of them.

"Let's get the hell out of here," Jock yelled at Dewey.

"Yeah, we're getting swallered up," Ringler said.

They were in danger now, Jock knew. Their horses were being jostled by huge bodies and raked by sharp horns. Both men fought free, slapping their hats against their horses' flanks and spurring them to outrun the maddened flight of cattle gone berserk.

Somewhere beyond the drag riders, Abel saw the dust cloud and heard the sound of bawling cattle. The ground seemed to shudder beneath his horse's feet as if he were riding through an earthquake. He slowed his horse and then came to a stop.

"A damned stampede," he muttered, and felt a swirling in his suddenly empty stomach.

From the sound of it and from the growing size of the dust cloud, he knew the stampede was a big one, involving, he was sure, some fifteen thousand head of cattle. And those cattle could run for a hundred miles and take days to find and run back into the herd.

Well, he was patient.

It was still a long way to Ellsworth, and

he would find Jock somewhere on the trail between here and there.

It was only a matter of time, and Abel had all the time in the world.

Chapter 26

It took the X8 hands two days to fully stop the stampede, and the hands spent most of another week rounding up strays, some of which had run forty, fifty, or sixty miles off course. Still, Jock kept the main body of the herd moving, for he knew that this would serve to calm them down. Chad was worried, though, and had slept little, as had many of the drovers, during and after the massive stampede.

"You need to learn how to sleep on horseback, Chad," Jock told him. "You look like a derelict."

"Sleep? What's that?"

"It's something that wipes those worry lines off your forehead."

"I think they're permanent, Jock."

"Well then, Chad, take some comfort out of that stampede. It wasn't all bad."

"No? I could lose a thousand head or more."

"You won't lose that many. Might not lose any at all."

"Where's the comfort? We got hands scattered from hell to breakfast rounding up strays."

"We gained some miles, Chad. Most of the herd, trained as they are, stayed to the trail. Sometimes I think they already know the way to Ellsworth."

Chad snorted, but he smiled, too. "Yeah, we did gain some ground, all right, Jocko. Left old Torgerson, that conniving, evil-hearted bastard, in the dust."

It was true, Jock thought. They had not lost any more men since the hanging, and he no longer had to send out scouts since they had taken care of the Apaches, whom he was certain had been sicced on them by Torgerson. At last sighting, Torgerson and his herd were well behind them and way off track.

But it was a long way to Ellsworth. They had many months of driving ahead of them and it would probably be winter before they got there. For now, it was high summer and the herd was moving well, with the leaders reestablished in their customary positions. There was a contentment among the cattle that could be seen in the way they grazed and bedded down at night. Jubilee and Mac kept all of them well fed, with fresh calves to butcher and deals made to buy staples and vegetables from farmers and ranchers. It was a good life, he reckoned. Hard, but good.

They crossed the salty Brazos near Waco, and drove on to the Sabine through a driving rain and annoying winds that plagued the drovers worse than the flies and gnats. By the time they reached the crossing at the Sabine, it was impassable. The rains had swollen the river until it was over its banks, and the west wind drove the rushing waters into a speedy froth.

"Cap'n," Jesse Boyd said to Jock while they were waiting for the river to subside, "this might not be the time nor place, but Suzy Q wanted me to tell you something that might be important."

Jock had been hunting for a suitable ford all morning and his mood was as dark as the threatening sky. He knew there was a chance for more rain, and if so, they could be a week or two getting across the Sabine.

"Something wrong with the remuda, Jesse?" Jock said.

"No, sir. Suzy Q's doing just fine. So are the horses."

"Then, what is it?"

"Well, sir, he says there's been a rider dogging our trail for the past two weeks or more. Doesn't catch up to us, but just keeps on coming."

"And that has him worried?"

"Not exactly. It's just a pester to him, like a bodacious itch, you know."

"Well, I've got better things to worry about than a lone rider way down the line."

"Cap'n, it just didn't look right to me. I mean, there's better places to go than to follow a pile of cow turds and grass eaten down to the scruff. When a man rides by hisself he sometimes seeks a little companionship, and this trail ain't exactly Fort Worth."

"No, it isn't. Well, I can't be bothered with a trifle like that just now. I've got men strung out all up and down this damned river looking for a ford, and we keep coming up with a moving ocean at every damned likely spot."

Jock looked up at the sky, then back down to Jesse Boyd, his face contorted with the annoyance he felt inside.

"I took it upon myself, Cap'n, to do a little reconnoitering, just to put Suzy Q's mind at ease."

"What did you do, Jesse?"

"I laid back for a couple of nights. Drifted real slow to the south until I got behind this jasper. I borrowed a spyglass from Jubilee one night."

"So, what did you find out, Jesse?" Jock tried to be patient with the young man, but it was a real chore under the circumstances.

"Well, sir, I stayed way out of sight, but I put that spyglass on him and studied him for the better part of two whole days."

"Did you find out what he was up to, Jesse? Was he a bandit, a rustler?"

"I don't rightly know his purpose, Cap'n, but I recognized him. I seen him when he come to Mr. Becker's ranch looking for a job. Him and them two rowdies you hanged a while back."

Jock felt as if a hammer had been cocked in his brain. A sudden jolt of electricity sparked a warning deep in his mind. He was already soaking wet, but now he felt cold and clammy, as if somebody had walked over his grave.

"Abel?" Jock said.

"Yes, sir, your brother. I seen him real plain."

"What in hell is Abel doing following us?"

"I don't rightly know."

"Did you tell Suzy Q who it was you saw, Jesse?"

"No, sir. I come right straight to you."

"Thanks, Jesse. You keep that information to yourself. Where is Abel now? Do you know?"

"I reckon he's keeping his same distance, though I can't rightly say. It took me a good half day to ride up here from where Suzy Q was wrangling the horses up to the river, what with the rain and all."

Why was Abel following the X8 trail? Did he have a rift with Torgerson? Or was he working for Torgerson, up to no good? And why all the secrecy? If Abel had a purpose, so far he hadn't shown his hand.

"He must be living off the land," Jock said aloud. "He knows how. My pa and I taught him everything we knew."

"He's eating right good, Cap'n. I saw him pick up a stray calf and cut its throat, skin it out. He eats right well, I'd say."

The sky got even darker and in the distance there was the rumble of thunder—an ominous sign on a day when the river was roaring by in full race. More rain would only make it harder to cross.

"You go on back to work, Jesse," Jock said. "I'll take care of Abel."

"Yes, sir. I hope I done right, telling you what I seen."

"You did. Keep your slicker handy, son."

Jesse saluted and turned his horse. Jock watched him ride away and thought some more about his brother. Abel was up to something, that was certain. But what? If he had wanted to join the X8, he had had plenty of opportunity. No, he was up to no good. The problem was that Jock didn't know what was on his brother's mind. Not yet. But he was determined to find out.

Chad and Dewey rode up a moment or two later.

"What did young Jesse want?" Chad asked. "He's supposed to be helping Suzy Q with the remuda."

There was nothing to tell Chad, Jock reasoned. Nothing that would not worry him needlessly, and more than he worried now.

"I'm going to have to ride back and take a look at the remuda," Jock lied. "Suzy Q sent Jesse to get me."

"Oh, what's the trouble?"

"I don't know exactly. I won't be long. We can't cross this river now, so just tell everybody to sit tight. I'll be back by morning."

Chad didn't protest. Jock didn't give him time. He turned his horse and rode south, a plan forming in his mind. Along the way, he thought about Abel and felt a little guilty that he hadn't paid more attention to him after their parents died. He had been so devoted to Twyla and so stung about losing that herd that he had let his little brother run wild. It was no wonder he had taken up with those two wastrels, Randy and D.F. It was no wonder that he had looked for excitement away from their ranch and had fallen in with bad companions.

His anger at Twyla's death had subsided a great deal on this drive. He had had time to think it through. Life was such a funny thing, he mused. It could neither be planned nor measured. Sometimes the good died young. For no reason. Sometimes life made no sense, and Twyla's death had seemed like the end of the world to him. But now he had distance between her death and the present. The herd, the drive, that was what gripped him now. That was his new love, perhaps his destiny. In looking back, one could see all the twists and turns in life, but one could never see the future. Who was to say that Twyla's death was not meant to be? Perhaps that was her destiny, and perhaps her death had been preordained so that he could go on living and regain something he had lost. Life was a puzzle, all right, and Abel had taken his twists and turns, as well. Like a blind man. Like Jock himself. Both of them groping through the dark, both angry, both laying blame when perhaps neither of them was the target of the other.

It was a long ride, past a long line of cattle all bunched up like people waiting in a queue to board a ferry that would take them across the river high and dry. And where was he going? Jock wondered. And what would he do when he got there? What would he say to Abel? What would Abel say to him?

Thunder boomed softly in the distance and the heavy black clouds seemed to press down on him as Jock swung wide, away from the herd. He knew now what he was going to do. He rode well south and then doubled back at a place where he figured Abel had already passed. He wanted to come up behind him, perhaps catch him unawares before either of them made a mistake they both would regret for the rest of their lives. He was looking for tracks, tracks of a horse among the maze of hoofprints. The light was dim and the way uncertain.

But it was something he had to do. It was

something he hoped would straighten out some of those twists and turns in his and his brother's lives.

Jock prayed, then—prayed that he could find the tracks on this blackest of all days.

He prayed that he could find his way in the darkness of that somber day.

Chapter 27

Jock saw it as a tiny flicker of light in a pool of darkness.

A campfire.

The night had come on so subtly that he had not noticed it at first, until his eyes began to burn from trying to see the tracks. He had found them, almost miraculously, among the myriad of cattle and horse tracks that marked the progress of the passing herd. They were the freshest and, to his experienced eye, they stood out among all the others. Abel's tracks. Tracks made by a horse Jock knew. A horse with a peculiar gait. A horse that dragged his right hind hoof like a tentative brake when it was tired and wanted to stop and rest.

The campfire was an encouraging sight. It meant that Abel had stopped and made camp for the night. He would be there. And perhaps he would not be expecting company.

Jock rode very slowly as he drew closer to the small, blazing fire. He could smell meat cooking. He did not roll or light a cigarette, though his nerves demanded that comfort.

He slowed his horse even more when he made out Abel's silhouette by the dancing flames of the fire. Abel's back was to him. He sat facing north and he held a stick in his hand that was skewered into a chunk of calf meat. Jock could smell the calf's entrails, the tang of spilled blood, the aroma of blood-wet cowhide.

"Got enough grub for two?" Jock asked, startling his brother.

Abel dropped the skewered meat into the fire and picked up his rifle, which was leaning against his saddle, close at hand.

"Put the rifle down, Abel. You won't need it."

Abel turned and looked up at his brother. Jock held his own rifle and it was leveled at Abel's chest.

"You going to shoot me, Jock?"

"No. I came to talk."

"Talk? What about?"

"About you and me. I've got coffee in my

saddlebags. It would go good with that beef you're cooking."

Abel set his rifle back down, leaning it against his overturned saddle. Jock slid his own back in its sheath.

"Light down, then," Abel said, a sullen tone to his voice. He picked up the stick and lifted the cooking meat from the fire. "I got enough calf meat for both of us, I reckon."

Jock swung down, ground-tied his horse to a creosote bush and walked over to the fire, then squatted down to face his brother. He carried a tin of coffee, a pot, two tin cups and his canteen.

"Coffee would be good," Abel said. "I ain't had none for weeks."

"I'll set the pot on to boil."

The two men sized each other up and Jock rolled a cigarette, which brought a faint smile to Abel's lips.

"Want me to roll you one, Abel?"

"I wouldn't mind. I can roll it myself. I run out of tobacco two days ago."

"I think we've both run out of a lot of things," Jock said.

"Huh?"

"Words, for one thing. Apologies. Explanations. The past. People we loved and cared about."

"You want me to apologize?" There was a hostile edge to Abel's tone of voice.

Jock pulled out the makings and slid two papers out of their packet. He shook his head.

"No, Abel. The other way around. I don't blame you for Twyla's death. She had a bad heart. She could have gone at any time. We both knew that. Doc Ford told us both that much."

"I didn't mean to hurry it none, Jock."

Jock filled the papers with tobacco.

"I know. Look, it was a tough situation and it's happened before. Two men want the same woman. We were way out on the ranch, away from town. Liquor works funny things on a man's mind sometimes. I'm sorry Twyla died, but I don't blame you."

"You don't?" Abel looked genuinely aghast, with his jaw dropped and his mouth gaping open.

Jock handed a paper with tobacco to Abel, unfolded. Abel rolled it up and licked the edge to seal it. Jock did the same with his cigarette. Then he pulled a flaming faggot from the fire and lit Abel's quirly, then his own. The two men smoked in the ensuing silence.

"No, Abel, I don't. You can't brand a man for life because of one mistake, or just one thing he might have done."

"I didn't know you felt that way, Jock. I made a mistake. I'm still sorry about it."

Jock waved a hand in the air as if to wipe away Abel's guilt.

"I know you are. It's gone, Abel. Forgotten."

"Maybe I should do the same with my friends, Randy and D.F."

"What do you mean?"

"You killed them, Jock. My best friends. I'm still mourning for them."

"I didn't kill them, Abel. Curt Torgerson killed them. Sure as he sent them to kill X8 hands, he sent them to their deaths."

"I come to kill you, Jock."

Jock blew a thin stream of smoke out of the side of his mouth and looked down at the ground.

"I figured as much, Abel. Now you have to ask yourself a question."

"What's that?"

"When I came up on you a little while ago, you had your back to me. I had my rifle in my hand, cocked and ready. I could have shot you in the back and nobody would have been the wiser."

"Why didn't you, Jock?"

"Then Torgerson would have had another notch on his gun without ever dirtying his hands."

"You put it that way, I guess I see your point."

"Those boys, Randy and D.F., they didn't know any better, living the way they did. But you were brought up different. You know right from wrong. You're young and you have your whole life ahead of you. It would be a shame if you died like they did, way before your time."

"Like Twyla," Abel mused.

"No, it was Twyla's time. In fact, she was living on a lot of it she borrowed. But you have your health and your youth. You know, the folks left that ranch in Del Rio to both of us. To you and me."

"What? I didn't know that. I thought they gave it to you because you were the oldest."

"Not so. Half of it's yours, Abel. If you want it."

Abel smoked and shook his head, his mind teeming with new thoughts.

"I don't really deserve it, Jock. You worked it. I just ran around with those boys and got into trouble."

"Think about this, Abel. I lost everything I

have. This drive is a new chance for me. It can be a new start for you, too."

"What do you mean?"

"Chad's made me a pretty good offer if I bring this herd into Ellsworth ahead of Torgerson. It means we can build our own ranch. You can find a girl and get married. Maybe I'll even marry again. There's plenty of room for both of us. You finish this drive with me and we'll be brothers again. Partners, too."

Abel thought about Jock's offer. Then he grinned and stretched out a hand.

"I'll ride with you, Jock. You won't be disappointed, either."

They shook hands.

"Coffee's boiling," Jock said. "Are we going to eat or sit around jawing all night?"

Both men grinned and shook hands again.

"Damn, Jock. I had you figured all wrong. I thought you were going to kill me for . . ."

"A man shouldn't fight when his temper's flaring like the morning sun," Jock said. "He should give it some thought first. I've had a lot of miles to think back on what happened, and I was wrong to run you off like that."

"I was wrong in wanting to take Twyla against her will. I had too much whiskey in me."

"Let's see how we both work with patches

on us, Abel. Ride with me to Ellsworth and see if life doesn't change for you and me."

"I'll do it," Abel said, and started cutting up the meat while Jock poured hot coffee into the two tin cups.

They were a week getting across the Sabine because it did rain again, but from then on the herd moved slowly and deliberately up the trail. Everyone was surprised to see Abel join the X8 hands, but Chad was grateful, for he was a good hand and more than earned his pay.

They crossed the Red, the most formidable river of all, and lost a few head, but Chad was both pleased and relieved to put that river behind him.

When the herd finally reached Ellsworth, he was surprised to find out that the townsfolk viewed him as a hero. The people cheered when they saw the huge herd fan out on the plain. Buyers rushed up to make offers and men slapped him on the back, then took him to fancy dinners with wine and champagne and expensive cigars to curry his favor.

But Chad was unable to eat the fine foods and he did not drink the wine or champagne. In fact, he did not imbibe any strong spirits whatsoever. For, shortly after they reached Ellsworth, Chad doubled over in pain and Jock took him to see a sawbones, who examined Chad and then read him chapter and verse. Chad was told that unless he changed his diet, he was going to die. The doctor told Chad he could not eat fried foods for six months, and prescribed a diet of boiled chicken, soft fruit, and plenty of dairy. Chad grumbled, but his health immediately began to improve.

Chad sold the herd to the eastern consortium that had originally approached him. They paid him a dollar a head more than the agreed-upon price. The drovers shared in the excitement and there were plenty of glitter gals to go around.

After Chad paid Jock and the men off, he met the stage and greeted his wife, Rachael, and his daughter, Victoria. While Victoria was glad to see Jock, her eyes were on Abel. And Abel, for his part, was smitten on the spot.

Jock found Lou Quist in one of the saloons, his head wreathed in cigar smoke, a girl in his lap. Jock handed him a sheaf of greenbacks.

"That's what I figure I owe you, Lou. With interest. I paid off the others who lost out on my drive, too."

Quist stood, and the girl bumped onto the bench in the booth with a startled look on her face.

"I had you figured wrong, Jock. Thanks. You're a good man to ride the river with, you know?"

"So are you, Lou."

Later, they heard that Torgerson had lost a third of his herd crossing the Red. He had tried to beat Mother Nature and Mother Nature had won. The river had been swollen when he started his herd across and the undercurrent swept cattle away like leaves in a windstorm. They also herd that a Kansas farmer had him thrown in jail for a month, and by the time Torgerson got out, more of his herd had vanished, and not a few had been slaughtered by irate farmers who blamed Texans for the tick disease that decimated their own domestic herds.

When Torgerson finally reached Ellsworth, the price for Texas longhorns had dropped and he barely made expenses. He got drunk and was thrown in jail there, too, and was all alone after his men rode back to Texas without him.

"I'm going to split the money Chad gave me with you, Abel," Jock told his brother.

"But I won't give it to you until we get back home to Del Rio."

"Why? Afraid I'll spend it?"

"Frankly, I'm afraid someone will steal it from you."

"Well, that's fine with me, Jock. I figure we'll put our money in one basket anyway, and rebuild our ranch. That's what I want to do with my share, anyway."

"Brother, you've grown up," Jock said.

"I've got plans. With Vicky, I mean."

"Vicky?"

"Victoria. We've been spooning, Jock. When I get back I'm going to ask her to marry me. Once we get the ranch going and all."

"That's fine, Abel. She'll make a good wife."

"And I'll make her a good husband, too."

Abel was grinning.

"Yes, you will," Jock said. "I know you will."

Jock rolled a cigarette, lit it and let it dangle from his mouth. The smoke stung his eyes, but Abel knew that wasn't the reason his brother had tears running down his face.

"What are you bawling for, Jock? Don't tell me it's the smoke."

"No, it's not," Jock said. "I'm just real happy, that's all."

"Happy about what?"

"I've just seen my baby brother grow up to be a man," Jock said, and turned away, embarrassed and choked up, ashamed to be seen crying openly in public.

Then Abel started to cry, sniffling and wiping his eyes, trying to quell the rush of tears.

"What in hell are you crying about?" Jock asked.

"I'm happy, too, Jock."

"About Vicky?"

"Yes, but about you, mostly. I'm glad I found a brother I thought I had lost forever. Damn, I'm a real happy man."

And so were they both, Jock and Abel, and they would become even closer on the long ride back to Texas, with Chad, Rachael and Victoria for company along the way.